GHOSTLY TALES OF THE BLACK HILLS AND BADLANDS

D0096190

Ghostly Tales

of the Black Hills and Badlands

Ruth D. Hein

Ruth D. Hein

Enjoy ghost hunting!

North Star Press of St. Cloud, Inc.

Printed in the United States of America by Versa Press,
Inc., East Peoria, Illinois.

Published by
North Star Press of St. Cloud, Inc.
P.O. Box 451
St. Cloud, Minnesota 56302

*This Book is dedicated
to all who helped me find these ghost stories
from the Black Hills and Badlands,
areas I have come to know better
because of their help.*

Acknowledgments

THANKS ARE DUE TO ALL those who gave me leads to the stories.

Several people who each helped me find more than one story were Marlene Wolf, Wall; Olivia Felder, Rapid City; Evelyn Mason, Lead; and the management and housekeeping staff at the Bullock Hotel, Deadwood.

Individuals who each helped with at least one story are Tony, "Jane," Angela, Jessica, and "Tracy," whose full names are purposely withheld; also John Paulsen; the Hoffmans, Shearers, and Crews; Jack and Cherrylee Bradt, of Rushmore Resort and Campground; a bell captain at the Franklin Hotel in Deadwood; Harry Lehman, of the House of Roses in Deadwood; and employees and former employees (or their relatives) of the Homestake Mine and Homestake Hospital—especially Mary Beauvais of Sturgis and Betty Dunn of Lead for details for the story about "Sally."

Staff writer Jamie Neely wrote the September 18th story about the Homestake Theater for the *Rapid*

vii

City Journal. The copy sent to me provided much of the information used in two stories about the theater's "spook." Thanks for that help.

If I have omitted a name, I apologize. Many interviews, letters, and phone calls led to many others, and I may have inadvertently forgotten someone who helped along the way.

Many thanks, also, to the publisher, editors, and others for taking on the project and for helping the stories materialize into this book.

Introduction

MY SHORT, EARLY OCTOBER VACATION with my husband Ken had a two-fold purpose. We were taking some time off, after a busy summer of outdoor work on our acreage, and I was to collect more ghost stories from the Black Hills and Badlands for this book.

The collection came together. There are plenty of stories out there. I asked a lot of questions and, fortunately, made contact with some key people who were in community services and tourism or who knew someone who had lived in the area for a long time and might know someone with a story for me.

The Badlands and Black Hills are very different from southwest Minnesota where we live, and from large parts of other states surrounding South Dakota—even the eastern part of that very state.

As I rode along in the passenger seat, watching maps and roadside signs, I happened to look ahead and upward. There, "in the sky," slightly to the right and ahead on I-90, I saw something unusual.

Who hasn't, as a child, watched the clouds take on shapes of animals, familiar persons, trees, or other objects? In this case, most of the clouds lay or floated horizontally, but off toward our destination an upright column of cloud separate from all the others drew my attention.

It wasn't exactly a column. It looked almost like a ghost. If it represented a ghost, then it appeared to be a woman's ghost, perhaps, or that of an elderly man with long, white hair and possibly wearing a loosely draped white garment that hung down to his or her feet.

Its posture suggested humility or weariness or maybe an apologetic mood—it was hard to say which from that distance. I looked up many times while, between glances, I made notes and tried to sketch what I saw. The filmy, draped figure remained in the sky a long time, against the faded gray-blue sky, and it seemed to be facing toward me, as if welcoming me and inviting me to proceed with my mission.

I looked up again and again. The more I looked, the more I saw. Behind the figure there was a less defined, less shapely whitish mass—somewhat shorter but with the appearance of movement, as if someone or something had emerged from it. Between the two cloud-film masses was a barely visible streaking of white in horizontal bands.

We were at least sixty miles from Chamberlain and would not reach the Badlands until the middle of the next day. But we were on the way, heading toward our destination. This upright column of cloud was the only thing like it in our entire view. Was it a sign? Did it mean I would find the stories I needed, to complete this collection?

I took it as such. We kept going west to the hills. Once we were there, the stories came to me, and I am grateful to all the storygivers for their help.

Background

THE DAKOTAS HAVE A COLORFUL HISTORY, a good background for ghost stories.

South Dakota became a state in 1889, the fortieth state to come into the union. Its lateness in doing so was largely due to its late settlement, after rail lines were extended and Indians gave up their land and were concentrated on reservations. In the early 1900s, settlement by whites picked up.

Before that time, gold had been discovered in the Black Hills in the summer of 1874. Prospectors and fortune-seekers rushed in, and many "boom towns" developed. The discovery of the Homestake Ledge or "lead" in 1876 resulted in the building of Lead City, now simply called Lead.

The state suffered during the drought, grasshopper invasions, and low farm prices of the 1930s (called the "Dirty Thirties" because of the dirt that blew and piled up) as did its neighboring states. South Dakota has long been an agricultural state, but recent changes have increased tourism and manufacturing. Commercial and industrial growth also occurred and mining became important.

The Black Hills in the western third of South Dakota are spoken of as well-eroded mountains. Harney Peak at 7,242 feet is the highest point in the United States east of the Rocky Mountains. The Black Hills and much of the western part of the state are wooded with national forests and are a source of a number of minerals. These include gold, silver, mica, beryl, uranium, lignite, and petroleum. The Homestake Mine at Lead is the largest gold mine in the Western Hemisphere.

In 1942 the sculptured monument displaying the features of Washington, Jefferson, Lincoln, and Roosevelt carved on Mount Rushmore by Gutzon Borglum was opened to public viewing.

East of the Black Hills is Badlands National Park. According to Ted Hustead's history of the Badlands in the Wall Drug brochure, the Badlands deposits once covered more of the area surrounding the Black Hills. Rivers flowing east from the hills, with the help of the weather, carried away sedimentary deposits. The process of erosion continues.

To preserve about a tenth of the White River Badlands, the area was made a national monument in January 1939. In 1976, 133,000 acres (the Stronghold Unit) were added. In 1978 the Badlands National Monument became a national park that covers 244,300 acres of the White River Badlands.

The "castles, walls, and statues" in the Badlands remain because erosion left only the hardest sandstone. Many fossils from the area have been placed on exhibit by the South Dakota School of Mines and Technology. They can be seen at the Museum of Geology in Rapid City.

The level, fertile land within the Badlands has been occupied by Native Americans, white homesteaders, and descendants of the settlers. The land of the Dakotas as a whole has been used by French fur trappers, Indians, soldiers, miners, cattlemen, and homesteaders.

Forty years of struggle between the white men and the Indians ended in the 1890 Wounded Knee Massacre that followed shortly after the Ghost Dances. The causes of the Sioux outbreak of 1890 are given as unrest due to the decay of the old life, repeated breaking of government promises, and near starvation.

The bison, the prairie, and the horse on which the Indians and early settlers depended were replaced by cattle, wheat, and gasoline-powered equipment.

After Wounded Knee, the Lakotas were confined to reservations for a time, but the arrangement didn't last. Since then, the Lakotas have increased rapidly to a larger population, and, I am told, that eighty-five percent of them live in cities.

The feature film *Dances With Wolves*, filmed in South Dakota, was set in the 1860s when the whites had started to move west to settle on the land of the Native Americans. In 1989 Kevin Costner directed, co-produced and starred in the film. The crews finished their work and left the area, but the plains, badlands, and canyons are still as they were during the filming and pretty much as they were in the years before the settlers disrupted the lives of the native Americans and the bison about 130 years ago in Dakota Territory.

The filming of *Dances With Wolves* came to be accepted by the Lakotas because they saw that it was authentic. It showed them as a proud people with complex personalities and endearing characteristics, with a capacity for friendliness, compassion, love, humor, and the ability to understand and to get along. Their dancing, singing, and extended family concepts were also depicted in the film with authenticity.

North Dakota also became a state in 1889, the thirty-ninth in order of admission. Rising above the drift plain 300 to 400 feet, the Missouri plateau lies diagonally in a northwesterly to southeasterly direction in North Dakota.

West of the Missouri River is the Missouri slope with the badlands of the Little Missouri River. These North Dakota badlands have buttes and mesas, exposed layers of colorful clay and rough lava. Black Butte, 3,468 feet above sea level, is the highest point in North Dakota. The Theodore Roosevelt National Memorial Park of 70,374 acres is in the scenic badlands of the Little Missouri River.

Some of the stories in this collection take place in the badlands of North Dakota. All the others take place in the Black Hills and Badlands of South Dakota.

Homesteading in the Badlands

TO STEP BACK IN TIME AND GET THE FEEL of homesteading in the Badlands, one might make a stop at the Prairie Homestead at the northeast entrance to Badlands National Park, just off I-90.

On the National Register of Historic Places since Spring of 1974, Prairie Homestead preserves the way of life of the sodbusters. It also sets the mood for several stories in this collection that took place on Dakota homesteads of the early 1900s.

Homesteading came late in the western third of South Dakota because the Indians were reluctant to give up their land and their way of life and because the railroad hadn't yet come across the state. Though the area was surveyed in 1892, it wasn't settled until 1900 through 1913, after the Homestead Act was declared and was changed several times. Finally, only five acres had to be plowed into crops, and, if a homesteader had lived on the claim for eighteen months and wanted to purchase it, he could pay fifty cents an acre and receive a "patent" on the land.

1

The prairie homestead.

In 1909, Mr. and Mrs. Ed Brown homesteaded the 160 acres on which their original home still stands. Mr. Brown paid $80.00 for the land.

Later, the Crew family owned the site. Keith Crew said, "My folks homesteaded just a couple miles away, a year after the Browns did. Theirs was probably one of the many depressions in this area that are reminders of where families "dug in" to establish new homes and make new beginnings. But the place hasn't been preserved like this one has."

Ed Brown built his home using cottonwood logs and buffalo grass sod. A few years later, a deserted claim shack was brought in and added. It became the living room.

The chicken house and the cave for storing food were dug into the bank much as the house was. The sod house has specially constructed windows.

A brochure states that almost every 160-acre piece near the Pioneer Homestead has a side-hill depression where other early families "dug in."

At the Prairie Homestead, the buildings are still there. Furnishings and machinery are either original or typical of the time of the sod-busters. Memories are there for many who come back or just go to get the feel of life on the prairie a long time ago. There's an atmosphere that would be difficult to duplicate now, as if the ghosts of those hard-working settlers don't want people to forget the effort they made to settle the land.

Unmetered Lights

IF CONDITIONS AND OCCURRENCES on a place can lead to a haunting, then there is a farmplace about twelve or fourteen miles north of Wall that qualifies.

According to those who know this story, the house on the place was gradually being torn down by the owner. No member of his family had ever encountered a ghost or a presence there.

Although their son owned the farm later, Audrey and Maurice Hoffman lived on the place for about five years, from 1955 to 1960. Later, they lived a few miles farther north, at old Pedroe, beyond Creighton. But Audrey still knows about the type of unusual happening people noticed on the old farm.

"I worked at the Cactus Cafe at Wall for a while," she said. "I went right by the house often enough as I went back and forth to work. Sometimes I'd see lights on, sometimes not. No one was living there then, and there wasn't supposed to be anyone in there. Others saw the lights on, too."

4

Maurice's cousin, Walter Hoffman, knows the history of the house. From his home in Belle Fourche north of Spearfish he said, "There were three brothers: Dewey, Ben, and Walt Hoffman. Maurice was Dewey's son. I was Ben's son, so Maurice and I were first cousins.

"The house on that place," he continued, "was built in 1907, and Ben came in 1908. Uncle Walt came the year before. The house was one of the first ones built in that part of the country. By 1872 the railroad had come to the eastern part of the state, and once a bridge was built over the Missouri River, building materials were more and more available as the rails snaked closer our way. So that house was a two-story, frame structure."

Walter explained that the room where he himself saw lights on one night was the same room in which his Uncle Walt had died a few years earlier.

Walter said, "I was out plowing snow late one night when I saw an upstairs light on there. I went to get help. Together we went in and checked the house. We thought someone might be in there. We went upstairs and pulled the chain that turned off that light. We looked around outside, but there weren't any tracks in the snow. And we checked the pole, but the meter was gone! No meter, no power, yet lights!"

Dorothy Shearer, as a young girl, had stayed in that same house one night. She had been at her aunt's home nearby when they went over to the old place to kill and pick chickens. "Well," she said, "it started raining. And it kept on into the night—a regular thunderstorm! Everything was suddenly mud, and we couldn't get back to my aunt's house, so we stayed where we were all night. I was scared! I thought probably the lightning had frightened me, but maybe I had a sense of something not being right, there."

5

Walter told of another of his early experiences on the same old farmplace. He said, "When we were kids, we were afraid to stay there alone, even before our cousin was killed there. When there weren't any grownups around, we'd hear noises. It sounded like someone was walking around upstairs, or like floorboards creaking . . . you know how they do sometimes."

Maurice's father, Dewey, died on the place. He and Ben were out gathering cattle one day when Dewey stopped his horse, stepped down and died. "That would have been in 1954," Walter said. And there was no autopsy performed. It was presumed that he died of a heart attack. It was so sudden!

Walter's uncle Walt Hoffman moved onto the old farm around 1920. He lived there for a good many years, until about 1963 when he died of natural causes. It was during the latter part of that time that Maurice and Audrey also lived there and worked for Uncle Walt.

But during the earlier part of that time, Dewey's daughter Betty died there. Maurice said, "She was my sister, and she was only twelve. She was attacked and shot there. That was in 1936. She died there, in Uncle Walt's house.

"The person who was responsible was dead when he was found in the breaks (the rough country) not far from the place. The report was that he had killed Betty and left her there, then broke through the cedars into the breaks, and shot himself.

"When that happened," Walter said, "our dads went down there. That would be my dad and my Uncle Dewey. My older brother Sam and I went along. When they saw what had happened, Uncle Dewey was understandably upset to find his daughter there, just as she'd been left. He and Dad went to Creighton to call the law. I think they had the old crank phone system there yet.

6

"Sam found a roofing hatchet, and I found a claw hammer. We hid behind the front door. We didn't even know where the killer was. I wonder now what we thought we would do if he showed up.

"It seemed hours and hours that we waited for Dad and Uncle Dewey to get back. When they did, all of us had to wait for the law officers to come out from Rapid City before anything could be done. That took a while, too. All the while, we were pretty scared—but especially before our dads got back."

No one knows which of the players in the scene was turning on the lights, even when the power was off, and doing any other haunting that occurred there.

Was It a Battle Between the Wives?

KAREN HAD A JOB COOKING for the people who worked on the ranch. It was a busy cattle ranch in a valley not far from Buffalo Gap, and it took a lot of food to satisfy those men's healthy appetites after a day of outdoor work. Jenna helped Karen feed the men.

The big house was interesting enough in itself. When Jenna first went out to help Karen with the cooking, she found the two-story house was one of those well-built, beautifully furnished homes that would be great if only it were restored and then maintained. But no one had done that, and Jenna thought it was a shame. She could just picture that etched glass window and the fancy front door with its beveled glass pane . . . and the open staircase with its smooth, shapely banisters the way they must have shone in the early years when the house was well kept.

But now, the house was mostly needed as a place for feeding all the ranch hands. Its large dining room was the only suitable place. There was no room large

8

enough in the bunk house or any other building that was conveniently next to a kitchen.

Jenna soon learned that the present owner's first wife had died of natural causes, but that his second wife had died mysteriously. No one seemed to know why or how. Jenna thought maybe that had something to do with the eerie feelings she'd had when she walked into the house. Some of the younger hands told her they felt that way, too, when they were in the old house.

Apparently Karen felt that same eerie feeling, as well. At least, she didn't want to do the cooking all alone there in that big kitchen, with no one to keep her company while the men were all out on the land, so she talked Jenna into coming out to help her. Jenna was willing enough to come. Both girls liked to go horseback riding on the ranch, and they also liked to hunt with the pack horses in deer season.

So, it wasn't unusual that Jenna went out again to help Karen. When that day's work was almost over, Jenna realized that Karen had to cook the next day, too. Jenna said, "I can stay, but where will we sleep?"

Karen said, "Well, not in the bunk house, that's for sure. Let's try one of the big upstairs bedrooms. We have four choices."

Jenna chose one of the rooms and unrolled sleeping bags on the floor. They planned to get up and get everything done early the next day and have time left to hunt and ride in the evening.

Before they fell asleep, Karen told Jenna about the sounds she sometimes heard coming from the room in which they lay when she was working downstairs. She said, "Sometimes it sounds like someone's coming down the steps, but after three steps she stops and goes back up. And doors open and close up here, especially the closet doors in this room."

"Are you trying to scare me?" said Jenna. "And why did you say *she*?"

"I'm not trying to scare you," Karen assured her. "I'm just telling you like it is. This room used to be the owner's first wife's bedroom. If I have the closet doors over there shut when I'm up here, they'll be open again the next time I come up. Most of the spooky things happen up here in this room," she said. "And in the basement . . ."

"What's in the basement? I've never been down there."

"You don't want to go down there, either. You should see the weird floor. It's hardwood, and it's all heaved up like in big waves, but there's no water down there at all and no sign of the wood breaking away from the walls."

By now Jenna felt considerably alarmed. "Hey, forget it! I'll never get to sleep! Next you'll be telling me there's some weird creature living down there!"

Karen's eyes opened wide. "Yeah! A crocodile! No, I'm just kidding. I'll end my story right there!"

The next evening, after the men were all fed and the kitchen and dining room were straightened up, Karen and Jenna finally had their free time to go riding. Jenna was mulling what had been said the night before over in her mind, and they talked about the strange sounds and feelings and happenings. All they could piece together was that maybe the man's first wife resented his second wife and came back to express that resentment. Or, maybe it was his second wife who came back because she didn't like the way her life ended unexpectedly and mysteriously.

The two wondered where the rancher was for whom they were all working. Chances were he knew who the ghost was who walked the stairs and opened closet door. On the other hand, maybe he had good reason to keep his distance.

Let It Grow Grass!

JOHN PAULSEN SAID, "I spent five years in and around the Badlands during the Dirty Thirties, and the only thing I ever heard that came close to a ghost story was the one about the man down at Interior."

The Dirty Thirties to which John referred were the years in the 1930s when the dust storms hit the area. The wind blew so hard that it covered the fences with dirt and suffocated cattle because of the dirt in the air. Nothing would grow.

But that had nothing to do with the ghost story John went on to tell, except that he had heard it back then.

Along toward the end of the 1800s, a man by the name of William D. Rounds lived at or near Interior in the Badlands. This man had his own ideas about how the land should be used. His ideas weren't always in agreement with those of nearby homesteaders. While others worked hard to break up the hay bottoms and tablelands so they could raise a grain crop, Rounds just let the prairie grasses grow as tall as they could.

11

When anyone asked him why he wasn't out making a field ready for the next season, his ready answer was, "The good Lord made this 'ere country to grow grass, an' I hain't a gonna try ta persuade it ta grow nothin' else. Leave that fer Ioway and Minneesotay, or even Nebrasky er Kansas."

"You see," John said, "Rounds was a rancher. In those days, ranchers and farmers didn't get along. The ranchers didn't want their pasture land broken up to 'just farm.'

"Well, Rounds passed away sometime in the early 1920s and was properly buried in the cemetery at Interior, with a blanket of sod—real grass—to cover him. And that grass really did grow and grow and grow, surprisingly enough, since the soil wasn't very fertile there."

John said that the grave marker noted the man's birth and death dates and his full name, with his parents' names given briefly below his own. All was duly recorded there, although as early as the 1920s his death might not have been entered in the county recorder's office as is done nowadays.

The trouble came about fifteen years later. The townfolks from Interior went out to the cemetery to neaten it up that spring, one of the jobs to be done was the mowing.

The person who cut the grass had the most trouble. He found that he could easily enough guide the mower around the markers and between the rows. And he had no trouble mowing over the tops of the old, flattened or sunken graves or even over the still slightly mounded newer graves—except for one. Every time the caretaker or his helper tried to mow over the top of the grave in front of the tombstone identifying the burial place of "ROUNDS," the lawnmower would come to a dead stop!

Townspeople began to comment on what was happening in the cemetery. Some thought Mr. Rounds must still be around, and maybe he was jinxing the mowing equipment. Others said, "Why, it's just as if a stick or a wire or rod was stuck in the reel, but when you get down and look for it, there's nothing there but the blades."

The general conclusion drawn had to do with what Mr. Rounds had always said when he was alive. When people commented on that grass growing on that grave, they usually ended the discussion with, "He never did think the land should be expected to raise any other crop. Why, he never ever even owned a plow!"

"Let it grow grass," Mr. Rounds was saying in effect, whenever anyone approached his grave.

Disturbed Since the Flood

ON THE WEEKEND THAT DAVE AND SUE came to Rapid City to help Sue's mother, Arlene, pack up and move, they had no trouble finding her house. It stood at the corner of Castle Heights and Sheridan Lake Road right by Queen Heights, a short street in southwest Rapid City, just off Jackson Boulevard. The house had not always stood there. It had had a previous "life" in another part of town. But in 1972, after extremely heavy rains, with "absolute downpours" as some tell it, the runoff went straight through town and flooded everything there as well as areas in the hills, where residents and tourists died in the rampaging waters. Arlene's house had to be relocated after that.

About eight years later, Sue and Dave came to help Arlene move. After a day's work, the two young people lay on the living room floor, where they had made up a temporary bed. Their son Cory slept in the crib Arlene had kept handy for him. Still awake, Dave and Sue both heard muffled voices coming from the basement. Having been alerted to the fact that, according to the rest of the family, all sorts of weird things went on in that house, they listened to the voices. They could make out a few words better than others.

It sounded as if someone was trying to quiet someone else so that the people asleep in the attractive, comfortable, ranch-style house would not be disturbed. Dave thought he heard, "Shh . . . they're gonna hear us . . ." and Sue heard an almost distinct, "Quiet!"

That particular evening, what puzzled Sue and her husband about the sounds was that no one could possibly be down in the basement when they heard the voices. No one could get down there except by walking through the house and into the kitchen, where the door to the basement was located. And no one had come through that day or evening, except for Arlene's family, and they had all gone to bed.

The young couple lay quietly and listened for about five minutes, or at least it seemed that long to them. Suddenly they both heard a loud bang coming from the basement. Sue said later, "It didn't really sound like a gunshot, though I thought of that. It was more as if something made of wood . . . a clothes rack or some cleaning equipment . . . had fallen over. In a quiet house, that would make a loud noise, especially if it fell onto the cement floor. And since the basement was still unfinished, there was no carpeting to soften the sound."

Sue and Dave had been told about the muffled voices. They also knew that Arlene had found the basement door locked from the inside several times, when no one was down there and there was no way anyone could get into or out of the basement, unnoticed, to lock it. Another weird thing about the house was that Arlene's son, Mark, had reported hearing what sounded to him like chains rattling down the cellar.

Dave remembered that everyone got up—Arlene and Mark as well as her younger daughters, Carrie and Dessie. The children were, at the time, in fourth through eighth grades. Arlene, a single mother not yet forty, had her younger children living with her after two marriages that had ended earlier.

The commotion of everyone getting up and milling around, asking, "What was that noise?" and "Why are you guys up?" and "Who turned all the lights on?" was enough to waken young Cory, about six months old. He set up a howl as he was roused from sound sleep by the total turmoil.

Dave said, "Someone grabbed a baseball bat, and we all went down the cellar steps. There, we found that a broom had fallen over, but not along the wall where it usually leans. We found it in the center of the floor of the wide-open basement!"

Sue, trying to quiet Cory by gently rubbing his back as she looked for his pacifier, said, "That broom must have been thrown hard by *someone* or *something* to land in the middle of the floor like that. A broom can't propel itself that way, or glide from the wall to the middle of the floor and fall flat there!"

But no one came up with an answer, or even a reasonable possibility. That was in January of 1980.

Arlene recalled another day, quite a while earlier. She had driven to the school . . . a ten-to fifteen-minute run . . . to pick up her children at the end of their school day. They were ready and waiting, and they all headed home. When they reached the house and went in, the kids headed for the kitchen where they plunked their backpacks down on the counter. Then all three rummaged in the refrigerator and the cookie jars, looking for snacks.

Arlene headed for the bathroom, farther down the hall. She realized that the three cups of coffee she'd had with a neighbor just before she left for school made her trip to the bathroom urgent. When she got there, she was shocked to see something smeared on the bathroom walls and in the tub. It looked more like blood than anything else. It looked as if someone had smeared it on the wall purposely, or maybe had pawed frantically at the wall, trying to get out of the tub after an injury or whatever might have happened. And the tub was a bloody mess, too.

That was when Arlene remembered what she had heard earlier. She was told that someone had died in that very same house during the flood of 1972. After that flood, her house, along with a number of other houses had been moved from one of the lower, badly flooded parts of town to this area on Queen Heights Street. It became a housing project for low-income families. Here, the houses were all set on new, unfinished basements.

Arlene wondered what the circumstances of that death in the 1972 flood were. Had someone been trapped, unable to escape the house when the waters rose?

When Arlene went back to the kitchen, where the children were still enjoying their afternoon snack, they asked her if she wanted a peanut butter and jelly sandwich, too. All three wondered why she refused to join them at the counter. All she said was, "No, thank you! I'm not in the least bit hungry!" before she left to talk with her neighbor.

The conversation between the two women centered around the scene in Arlene's bathroom. Fran said, "There must have been someone in your house while you were gone. Is there anyone you know who might have a reason for doing such disturbing acts in your house . . . to get back at you for something, or whatever?"

Arlene said, "But no one was in the house when I left, and I had locked the doors. How could anyone get in, and why would they do something like that? And lately, the kids have been hearing muffled voices outside their bedroom windows, too, at night. What is all that about?"

Fran could offer no help. She had only heard rumors from Arlene herself about strange happenings in that house, like the muffled voices from the basement.

With Dave and Sue's help while young Cory either slept or was entertained by Dessie and Carrie, the packing up of the furniture, clothing, toys, and personal items was finished by Sunday evening. Arlene and her three youngest children moved out of the house shortly after that weekend, to one where no weird things had happened. Arlene said, "Apparently whatever was causing them—whether a ghost or spirit or poltergeist or whatever—didn't follow us. But I knew the woman who moved into the house shortly after we left, and I kept in touch with her. She, too, reported many weird things happening there."

A Silhouette at Dusk

EACH YEAR, WHEN THE LEAVES BEGIN to signal that autumn is coming, it's fairly easy to reflect on memories of childhood and youth. Angela said, "I often recall one of a mansion and a silhouette at dusk."

At just the right age, Angela became a Brownie. Her troop had campouts and did all the usual activities the leaders and their handbooks suggested.

When Angela was seven, her troop camped out overnight in a large wooded area with a grassy slope between the group campsite and a large house everyone around there called "the mansion." Because they were some distance from town and because several vehicles were needed to transport the troop and the equipment to the site, a couple of fathers went along as drivers and participants in their daughters' activities. The leaders themselves were mothers of the girls.

Once the camp was about ready—the tents set up and cooking gear set out—it was time for the girls to gather dry wood for their campfire. They had fun doing this, because they could roll it down the slope to one of the dads who was trying to build a campfire. Once the fire took hold, all the girls at a signal gathered around and settled in, "ready to hear the ghost stories," that were part of their agenda.

It was warm and cozy by the fire, and the young campers and parents were grateful for the warmth on that calm, crisp evening.

One of the leaders agreed to start the storytelling with one of her own tales. As the girls listened, they saw a young woman, who was not part of their group, come down the slope from near the mansion. She walked very slowly toward the circle around the fire. As she approached and gracefully seated herself, the girls could all see her in the firelight. She was lovely, and—yes—young, "but not as young as us," Jennifer said later. Angela noticed how thin and pale she looked, and Sarah saw that she was wearing a ragged lavender dress with panels of worn-out lace in the skirt.

When the leader had finished telling her story, Sarah whispered very quietly to Jennifer, "That sounded a little too made up. Do you think it really happened?"

Before Jenn could answer, Angela hushed her. "Quiet. I think our guest has a story of her own to tell." Then, turning toward the young woman, Angela asked her, "I don't know who you are, but can you tell us a story? Maybe like what it would be like to live in the mansion? Do you live there?"

The young woman began, "Why, it is commonly known around here that no one has lived in the old mansion on the hill for many years. But I suppose the story does live on."

"What story? Tell us! Tell us!" came from the Brownies seated around the campfire, their faces and voices reflecting their eagerness to hear a new story.

Slowly and with great composure, the young woman told the story. In her soft, barely audible voice, she said, "Many years ago, a young couple moved into the house shortly after their marriage. All the neighbors thought they were very happy, being newly married and all, but no one ever saw them in town or out on their land. That seemed strange. Then, one night, the young mistress of the house was taking a bath when someone, thought to be a stranger at first, came into the room and axed her to death."

A circle of gasps broke the brief silence. Then she continued, "Neighbors heard nothing at all that night. But the next day, the gardener came to get the flower garden ready for winter. As he pulled up the bloomed-out annuals and mounded some earth around the base of each rosebush, he thought he heard someone moaning. Telling himself it was just the wind in the trees, he finished his work and left for home.

"Eventually, the bride was missed. Her body was found, and the authorities decided she had been murdered. Her husband was never found.

"From then on, every night, the neighbors heard unusual sounds coming from the mansion. People down here at the bottom of the hill would hear sounds echoing into the valley beyond the campground.

"Finally the butler was found. He was chopping away with an axe around the base of the chimney of the old house. They took him away forcibly. He never said a word about what happened earlier or why he was doing what he was doing."

While the storyteller paused for a moment, the girls clamored for more.

"All right. But my story is almost ended," said the young woman. Then she told them that the young mistress of the house still roams the rolling slope dressed in her burial garment. "As she moves about," she said,

21

"long wisps of tattered lace follow gracefully by her side. And wherever she goes, there are ghostly silhouettes of young girls following her. You will hear the gentle swish of her garments as she glides down to the cove down in the valley."

At the mention of "silhouettes of young girls," the members of the Brownie troop edged in closer to their leaders. They watched every move the thin figure made as she rose and politely thanked them for their company. As she faded away down the slope and into the night, the girls heard her gentle weeping. A soft breeze across the treetops in the grove seemed to whisper, "Beware . . . beware . . . beware." Yet the troop sat mesmerized by what they had heard and seen. They sat staring into the campfire and shivering, until Jenn's dad said, "Okay, now. You wouldn't be shivering if you'd go and get more wood for your campfire!"

And now, many years later, Angela remembers the legend about an old mansion on a hillside and a murder committed there. At dusk, especially in the chill of an autumn evening, she sees long wisps of tattered lace trailing down the hillside. The only difference is that now, in real life, no children follow the ghostly young figure down into the valley.

Mysterious Friend

THE UNPREDICTABLE DAYS OF WINTER cooperated with mild weather as we moved the last of the boxes into our "new" home. It was really an old house, but for us it was a new home. We had outgrown apartment living, and, when a friend told us he knew of a family that wanted to lease their home in the Rapid City area while they lived abroad, we made an appointment to meet with them.

I fell in love with the house the moment I walked inside. The entry revealed a brightly decorated dining room straight ahead, with a multi-colored Tiffany lamp hanging from the ceiling. To the left was an oak staircase leading to the second floor, where there were three bedrooms and a second bath. Scarlet-colored carpeting covered the floor in the entry and dining area. Just beyond the dining room was the kitchen with open cupboards, hooks for hanging skillets and pots, and a pot-bellied stove, which was the only heat source for the back portion of the house.

The kitchen range and tile-surfaced work unit stood in the middle of the kitchen. Directly behind the double sinks open steps led to the unfinished basement. One room on the main floor had not recently been redecorated. It was the parlor, directly to the right of the front entry. Old wallpaper, ripped and partially removed, draped loosely around the room. The front parlor adjoined a small living area that had been cozily redecorated. Wall-to-wall sliding wooden doors separated this living room from the dreary, cold, undecorated front parlor. The owners, Jonathon and Sarah, promised us that the front parlor would be repainted or repapered before they vacated the dwelling.

We agreed on the conditions of the lease and enthusiastically looked forward to the time we would take up residency in the charming Victorian home.

Moving heavy furniture and boxes is never much fun. I've never met anyone who claims to really enjoy it, but with the work of many hands, even the heaviest of burdens can be somewhat enjoyable . . . and so it was on our moving weekend. The time for which we had been waiting finally arrived when the day's work was done and it was time to relax and "settle in." We retired to the freshly made bed in the west bedroom on the second floor. We lay there quietly, listening to the peaceful stillness of the night, feeling totally content with the success of our move.

We talked about the events of the weekend and shared our feelings about how great it was to finally have the move behind us. I let my voice grow louder and louder as I said to my husband, "Earl, I feel such a sense of freedom that now we can be just as loud as we want. We don't have to worry about the tenants on the other side of the wall overhearing our conversations. We don't have to worry about playing music too loudly or talking too loudly and disturbing anyone." My voice was almost bellowing as I cheerfully expressed happiness over the privacy of living in a one-family dwelling versus apartment living.

My words came to an abrupt halt when a heavy barrage of sounds of slamming doors interrupted our new and briefly realized solitude. It was not the natural sound of doors opening and closing. As far as I know, it would not be possible for any door or doors to open and close in such rapid succession. It was incredible. I couldn't believe what I was hearing. I whispered to Earl, "Do you hear that?" He whispered back with a definite "Yes!" The rapid slamming lasted for about ten seconds.

We certainly didn't like the idea, but we knew we had to investigate. We carefully crept down the stairs, not knowing what we might find; but everything appeared untouched, and there were no signs of any activity.

We didn't spend much time puzzling over the "slamming doors incident." The next few days were spent putting things in their proper places. But then I was standing at the sink area in the kitchen one day when I heard a very loud, definitely mournful moaning coming from the basement. The open basement stairs opened directly behind the kitchen sink. Without any hesitation, I left the house and didn't return until Earl accompanied me. Again, we found no one there, and he tried to convince me it had probably been water pipes, the furnace, or something else mechanical, but I felt there had to be some other practical explanation. I refused to let it frighten me.

The next incident occurred when Earl was attending an evening meeting and left me home alone. I felt terribly uneasy on that particular night. I had grown accustomed to living alone and always believed (and still do) that by filling my mind with pleasant thoughts, there will be no room for unwelcome ones. But this night, it was different. I was not successful in trying to shrug off the horrible feelings of uneasiness. I cowered in the corner of the living area, watching television. The wooden doors that separated the living room from the parlor were closed because, even though that room had been elegantly redecorated, as Jonathon and Sarah had promised, it still felt cold and unwelcoming in there. I sat frozen in my chair, wondering when Earl would come home and hoping it would be very soon.

Finally, I heard the front door and knew that Earl had returned. That door had a deadbolt lock and carried with it a very definite and loud "*kerwump*" as the latch caught when the door securely locked in place.

I jumped from my chair and ran around the corner into the dining area that led to the front door. To my astonishment, Earl was not there, but, through the sheer curtains on the front door glass, I could see his pickup just pulling up at the curb in front. I ran outside to meet him, and we searched the house together. There was no one else there.

At first, Earl and I never talked about the possibility of another "presence" in the house, but there was some kind of unspoken realization that we were not alone. One day after we had lived there several months, I broke the silence by asking, "It's female, isn't it?"

With no further words of explanation necessary, Earl answered, "Yes."

He had had an experience with her that he didn't confide to me until much later. He had been in the attic admiring an antique carousel horse stored there. "It's beautiful, isn't it?" asked a female voice. Earl turned to the voice behind him, but no one was there. In remembering back, that must have been the day I wondered about Earl's very strange behavior. I was downstairs when I heard a lot of bumping and banging as he hurriedly scrambled down from the attic and second floor.

All the while he was calling to me, "Jeannie! Jeannie! Where are you? Jeannie!"

The initial events were, of course, startling. They took place very soon after we moved in. Over the days, weeks, and months that followed, we felt comfortable there, and there were no longer any threatening activities, except when we had certain overnight guests. That was when "she" performed in mischievous glory. I have often wondered if it was the power of suggestion. If guests came to our home after we had told them of our suspicions, they could have magnified perfectly normal house sounds, but there were some pretty odd occurrences. My niece and her friend claimed that she pranced around the rollaway bed in the parlor while they were there and laughed at them. My sister said she saw her leaning over my teenage nephew while he slept on the sofa in the living room downstairs. My mother said she thumped her on the head and visited my father in the bedroom upstairs. They all had their stories. My brother-in-law didn't share a story, but he started bringing his motor home with him whenever he came to visit, and wouldn't sleep in the house.

Eventually, we made inquiries into the history of the house. We learned that a young girl who had lived there with relatives had died of an illness. We never learned any further details.

Our first child, Erin LeeAnn, was born while we lived in this home. Baby Erin slept at my bedside for weeks before we put her in the nursery to sleep alone. I felt silly about my concerns and never discussed them with anyone, but I didn't know how our mysterious friend would take to having a new baby around. She certainly hadn't welcomed any of our guests in a very friendly manner. After a while, I sensed her acceptance of Erin and even wondered if she didn't help baby-sit at times. For example, my mother dozed off while holding newborn Erin and was awakened by a thump to her head. Perhaps our friend was merely trying to awaken Grandma so she wouldn't drop the baby.

I like to believe this spirit grew to accept us in "her home," and I even entertain the thought that she actually liked us. I sensed her presence in subtle ways at times, almost like the passing of a gentle spring breeze carrying the delicate fragrance of fresh flowers.

After three years, Jonathon and Sarah returned. Upon our first meeting, a small truth was confirmed. Jonathon was standing on a ladder, bringing down boxes they had stored in the attic. He turned and smiled down at me from his ladder and asked, "Did you notice anything particularly strange in the house?"

"Now you tell us!" I replied.

"Sarah even saw her once," he told me. So, my sister had not been exaggerating. I had always wondered why my sister should get to see her, but I did not. I'll probably never know why she came to each of us in a unique way. Some only heard sounds, some sensed a presence, some saw her. Does the strength of our various senses or sensitivities determine the manner in which these mysterious forces are revealed?

Shortly before the lease agreement terminated, we prepared to move out of our home. I didn't want to leave. The house had served us well, and I loved it dearly, inside and out. Our mysterious friend didn't want us to leave, either. I could sense that it was very difficult for her to let us go. Again, as they had when we first moved in, odd things ocurred when we started packing and moving. This time, however, there was physical evidence of damage. The chandelier in the entry partially fell and dangled loosely from the ceiling. Some interior walls cracked, and a portion of kitchen shelving toppled when no one was present. A few cups and saucers were broken as a result.

At dusk on a cold, wintry February day, I last witnessed her displeasure over our leaving. As I looked back at the house, it seemed to be breathing, expanding and contracting, and I sensed she was having one super temper tantrum.

When I was asked to write this account, I spent much time thinking about the how and why of it all. I will try to gather more informtion about the past occupants of the house, and especially the young girl who lived there and died over a hundred years ago.

The house has since been sold. The new owners have completely renovated the dwelling. Occasionally, I slowly walk by the house and wonder if the spirit of that young girl is still there. I hope she has now found the eternal place of peace. I will never forget her. I wish she had a name, but for now and until we learn more, I'll just call her our "mysterious friend."

"Jeannie"

A Lingering Presence

THE HOUSE OF ROSES IN DEADWOOD is a Victorian mansion on the National Register of Historic Homes. Located at 15 Forest Avenue, it stands high on the sidehill overlooking Deadwood's Historic Main Street. Its twenty-seven rooms are home to Victorian furniture and antiques from the 1800s and, it seems, more.

When Harry Lehman, the owner at the time this story was told, first moved in about twenty years before, he proceeded to restore and furnish the house. Something puzzled him, early on. He said, "The key-wound vintage clocks would not work. When I had them cleaned and checked, the clock doctor found nothing wrong with them. It was as if they just didn't want to work—almost as if they weren't quite satisfied with the way things were."

Up on third floor was an area that may have been servants' quarters in an earlier time. To Harry and the workers, the rooms were small and dreary with their windows boarded up. Harry said, "We put glass in the windows to let in the sunlight and to permit a view of the surrounding hills. Somehow—don't ask me how—that solved the problem with the clocks. We joked about it then, saying, 'The clocks must be happy now. They're working again.' But I don't know if the changes we made had anything to do with it."

If clocks have minds and feelings, perhaps that was it! At least, if they had been any of the original timepieces, they would have been more "at home" in the brighter atmosphere, more like in the years when the house was the social center for Deadwood's upper class who came there for elaborate parties and were at one time waited on by as many as twenty-seven servants.

Another puzzlement is the fragrance of roses lingering in some of the rooms. "And not just imagined," Harry said. "I've had a lot of ladies report that they smelled roses in here."

The house was built in the late 1870s. James Wilson started its construction in 1876. When his wife, Victoria Anne, joined him two years later, the house wasn't finished; it was not yet the "thing of beauty" it became. But Mrs. Wilson was grateful for the bank of wild roses outside. Perhaps because the roses "saved the day" for her, or maybe because she was fond of roses, she chose rose-patterned wallpaper for a number of rooms, and she had a rose garden planted nearby.

Harry said, "Sometimes ladies' groups take tours or hold events here. Some of them have reported smelling the fragrance of roses."

He added, "Men don't smell them. Women do. And you can ask Evelyn Mason. She commented that she smelled them. And I don't spray a rose-scented air freshener in the rooms just before tours, either."

Evelyn Mason, a historian who lived in Lead with her husband, Bob, at that time, has also seen a chair rock.

Harry explained that when workmen were doing renovations to restore the house—and since then, too, right up to the present—a chair has sometimes been seen rocking in one of the four second-floor bedrooms.

"A ghost finder who came in at my invitation felt a cold spot in the master bedroom, presumably the room in which the first lady of the house died," Harry said. "Her room was across the hall from the room where she is sometimes seen sitting in the rocking chair. A couple other women have also seen that chair rock.

"There's something else funny going on with the lights in the house," Harry said. "Sometimes they come on after I've turned them all off when I close the house for the night."

Harry told about the time he was already asleep when Phyllis Schoenfelder, a neighbor, phoned him. "It must have been after eleven, but I have a phone by my bed so I answered it right away. She said she saw a glow like lights on in the house and didn't see any sense in running up my light bill. Being retired, she was accustomed to being frugal.

"I told Phyllis to come on over, and we'd check it out. Together we walked through the house. In every one of the rooms, I had to turn the light on as we entered. But Phyllis was sure she had seen lights on before I turned them on!"

As they checked for lights, Harry was thinking about the party he had planned for two days later. Because he had a cold or flu-like symptonms or whatever, he was busy with the box of tissues all the while they went from room to room. He said, "I ought to get to work dusting the place to be ready for the party. The dust's starting to show on the furniture."

Phyllis joked, "Oh, don't worry about it. Maybe the ghost will dust it for you. It seems to like things bright and clean."

But Harry had no assurance that would happen. And he didn't quite feel like doing it himself, so he put it off. And as for the roses, although Phyllis mentioned that she could smell them just before she left, Harry couldn't smell them, for sure, with his head all stuffed up as it was.

The lights were eventually all off when Phyllis went home, and Harry went back to bed. The next day, he felt a little better, so he started to clean the house. He noticed that there was no dust to dust. Not even the bric-a-brac, knobs, or carvings on the antique pieces were dusty. With a forced-air furnace, even with filters, there normally would be dust. He thought, How foolish! I don't even like to dust. After all, it's not much fun. But I wouldn't have needed to, this time.

The day of the party arrived, Halloween. When the guests came, he still felt "a bit off," but the party had been scheduled, and people had paid for it. "By the way," Harry said, "some of those who came smelled the fragrance of roses."

Perhaps the ghost of Victoria Anne had come back to help get the house ready, since Harry didn't feel up to it. Maybe the rose scent lingered in the rooms she had cleaned.

When Harry had purchased the house, he had wanted it because there was room for his hobby, his antiques. He found out some of the history of the house. It had been built much like Victoria Anne's mother's home in Pennsylvania. After the great fire of 1879, it had served as a hospital while it was still very new. A lawyer and politician, James Wilson represented Dakota Territory and the young State of South Dakota in the United States Senate. His position probably made it possible for his wife to go to great lengths to get what she wanted. In furniture, for instance. To quote an Associated Press newspaper article (the name and date of the paper were omitted from the clipping), ". . . to get a piece of furniture, for example, Mrs. Wilson could have it carefully shipped by steamboat and wagon all the way from the East Coast." When she moved her belongings to Deadwood, they filled eight wagons of a 280-wagon train as it snaked westward across the prairie. She already had many fine pieces of furniture when she came to her new home.

But by the time Harry bought the house in 1972, it had changed hands many times and had been neglected for many years. Very little, if any, of the original furniture was left. Harry gradually furnished the rooms again with authentic period pieces, many of them found in other historic buildings in Deadwood and Lead. Some pieces have stories of their own to tell. In restoring the house, he had the good help of Victoria Anne's diary and records and the blueprints James had given to the archives in Washington, D.C. From these materials miraculously available, Harry knew that there was once a fifty-foot ballroom in the wing of the house that burned down ten or eleven years after the house had been completed. He also knew from her diary that Mrs. Wilson had a strong, vivacious personality.

According to her own entries, when she lived in the house and prepared for a party, she "went from room to room . . . an hour before the guests were expected. I did not leave all the responsibility to the servants. They had their own duties and were occupied in fulfilling them. I saw to little details, like picking up a rose petal that had fallen from an arrangement. I made a habit of setting the clocks so that they were all marking the time correctly, and, in general, I made sure the rooms were ready for our guests."

Harry said, "Now, when I get ready for a party, the clocks will start striking an hour before the arrival of the first guest. It's as if they want to let me know it's time to take that last walk-through to be sure I'm ready. When they chime, I know that either someone's coming or something's going to happen—in one hour!

"I know there's something funny going on with the clocks, because even the one I have purposely set so it won't chime will strike!"

Not only before parties but also at other odd times, the clocks will chime. "Basically," Harry said, "it's an hour before something happens—sometimes a major catastrophe like a big storm with electrical outages. Or sometimes before unexpected guests arrive, such as family members and other relatives."

Harry had this message for those who read this story: "As a matter of fact, I like getting company. It's a big house, so it takes tourists and friends and family visitors to help fill it and keep me company. This three-story wood structure set on top of a basement is open for free tours (but donations help keep the inhabitants happy) from 9:00 A.M. to 6:00 P.M. all year, or by appointment. Mrs. Wilson is long gone, but maybe you'd like to come to discover the lingering fragrance of the roses she liked so well, or observe the clocks' strange antics as she helps me prepare for a party. Or relax in the rocking chair when she isn't using it."

Harry added a final word: "The house is open on holidays, too. We try to arrange something special at special times. As it turns out, sometimes they are our best days! And I haven't told you all; there are some surprises waiting for you to discover for yourselves."

Lucky Pennies

IT SEEMS THAT THE GHOST HAS NOT LEFT the House of Roses in Deadwood. Harry Lehman, still the owner at the time of this writing, said that in early September 1997 one of his guests had experienced something very puzzling.

The house had temporarily become a "bed and breakfast" establishment, to serve as such for a week during the Sturgis bikers' rally, when housing for extra visitors to the area was very much in demand. Groups of bikers filled the bedrooms, some even slept on the floor in the living rooms. Others slept out in the yard, in tents or otherwise "out under the stars."

One morning, the ladies were at the kitchen table, having coffee and rolls, when one biker—I'll call him Walt—walked in through the back kitchen entrance. He and his wife had slept in a tent in the yard. Walt was surprized by a penny and a button hitting him as he came in. He was taken aback by that. Surely no one at the table had thrown anything. Walt couldn't figure out who threw the small objects, or why anyone would do that, so he talked to Harry about what had just transpired.

Harry said, "Well, we have a ghost in the house. Looks like the ghost didn't approve of something you did. Did you break anything or move something? The ghost doesn't like things to be destroyed or to be moved from their regular places."

Walt said he had done nothing like that. Having come in to take a shower, he went on upstairs to the bathroom where the claw-footed tub stood solidly on the floor. He removed his terry towel wrap, pulled the shower curtain hanging from the tub surround to one side, and was about to step into the tub when another penny hit him.

Walt puzzled over this. He knew it couldn't have been one of his biker friends. They were sitting out in the gazebo in the front part of the yard up on the hill, overlooking the sloping front lawn and the town down below. Nor could it have been his wife or any one of the other ladies. They had all left by then, to go shopping downtown.

Walt went ahead with his shower. Afterwards, he told Harry about this second attack by a penny.

Harry tried to make sense out of what had happened. He asked Walt, "Well, do you need money? If you do, the ghost could have been trying to help you."

As it turned out, though who knows how the ghost could have obtained this information, the couple did need money. They could have appreciated any help they could get about then, but they hadn't been talking about their new need very much. Shortly before the bike rally, they had lost their house in a fire in which their bike also blew up. They decided to go to Sturgis anyway, for a break and to get away from their problems. They rented the bike they were using.

Still trying to figure it all out, Harry took a good look at the two pennies. They were both the old wheat-back pennies with the sheaf of wheat on one side before it was replaced by the Lincoln head on later issues of pennies. Harry said, "I wish I had looked at the dates. Maybe that was significant somehow."

But Harry did check his own modest penny collection to see if any were missing. None were. Every penny was in its place in the rows in the folders.

Walt kept the two coins for good luck. He called them his lucky pennies. A few weeks after he and his wife returned to their home, he called Harry. He said, "Harry, we've found a suitable home. It was so easy. We got it just by taking over the payments on one that someone had to give up because of downsizing at his place of work. We're very satisfied with our new home."

Harry suggested, "Maybe you should be thanking the ghost!"

Lucky pennies, indeed!

Fright Left Them Speechless

"THE SOUNDS WOKE ME," SANDRA wrote to me. "They were unmistakable. The stairs in the old building creaked badly, and the doors squeaked loudly. There were a lot of doors, because Chase's had once been a hotel. On the second floor, while we lived up there, it had a forty-five foot long hallway with seven separate doors. Before that, there were even more, but through the years a few walls and doorways had been removed. We knew it had once been a hotel because room numbers were still visible on some of the doors.

"By the creaking I heard as I woke," Sandra went on, "I was sure someone was coming up the back stairs. Then, whoever it was opened the back door to the hallway. I assumed Ed had come back home for some reason, so I opened my eyes to greet him. He always came through the door by the bathroom, instead of going down the hallway that would bring him into the kitchen."

The building was really old—in fact, historic. Sandra and Ed Gerken lived there when Sandra heard

39

those footsteps in 1982. But she thought it odd that she had heard only three footsteps coming down the hallway after the back door had closed. She knew no one could take a step in that old building without making some kind of sound on the old wooden stairs and floors; only three steps would end up right in the middle of nowhere.

Sandra and Ed lived upstairs, on the north side of the two-story brick building. Ed's brother Don lived on the other side. Sandra was asleep in the third room back from Hill City's Main Street, and Ed had gone to work.

Lying on her stomach when the sounds woke her, Sandra was just about to call out Ed's name when she sensed someone standing at the side of the bed and leaning over her. She said, "I felt two legs pressed up against my right leg. Then I heard a very soft voice say, 'Excuse me.' I couldn't tell whether it was male or female. I tried to scream for Ed, but all that came out was a weak whisper and a mumble. No matter how hard I tried, I could neither yell out nor move.

"Realizing that someone other than Ed must be in the room, I forced myself to turn over and face whoever was there. I looked around. No one was there. I wasn't sure whether I felt relief or disappointment. I didn't know whether to laugh at myself for imagining things, or to cry because I was frightened. It was a really weird feeling not knowing what was going on."

Ed and Sandra knew that the old building had been a general store in 1908, possibly Chase's General Store. They had found a historic photo, dating back to that year, showing a sign reading "Chase's" above the front awning. The photo also showed several other Hill City buildings on the same street, some appearing substantial and permanent, others, smaller, resembling storage sheds against nature's background of hills. The

stores were of the era when wooden porches or boardwalks were raised above the muddy streets on blocks of
wood and one could easily approach the businesses from
the boardwalks and enter them under the protection of
the wide awnings.

The brick structure indentified as Chase's in the
1908 photo had endured from then, or possibly from
earlier, through the 1980s and still stands. Today, the
structure houses shops on the ground floor. The building's owner lives upstairs, in the apartment where
Sandra and Ed lived fourteen years earlier. There are
even fewer rooms and doors now because the entire
upper floor has been remodeled.

"I sat there," Sandra said, "thinking about all of
that and wondering, if there was a ghost whose spirit
haunted the old building. That evening, when Ed came
home, I told him what had happened to me. He didn't
have any helpful explanation at all, but he did reveal,
totally unexpectedly, that he'd had a similar experience
in that same room four years earlier, three years before
he and I had even met.

"Ed told me, 'I was in bed, too, when I felt a presence or something in the bedroom. I somehow got the
impression that it was the spirit of an old man maybe in
his seventies, maybe even older.'

"Then Ed said to me, 'I didn't actually see an
elderly gentleman, either. I just felt a presence. But it
gave me enough of a scare that I couldn't speak or move
for a while. When I could finally summon enough cour-
age to turn over and face my fear, I found only an empty
room staring back. No one was standing by the bed. No
one was floating through the doorway and down the
hall. And whoever or whatever it was that had startled
me, it must have left, but it made no sounds at all as it
went down the usually creaky steps, if that's where it
went. We may never know.'"

Unexpected Guests

A NUMBER OF UNUSUAL . . . one could say unexplainable
. . . incidents occurred in a house in Hot Springs while
Marlene Akhtar and her family made it their home.
Those incidents were reason enough for the Akhtars to
believe the house was haunted, perhaps by the ghosts
of occupants and guests from many years earlier.

Why guests? Because the house, long called the
Villa Theresa Guest House, was built by Fred T. Evans
in 1891 as a retreat for wealthy businessmen from Iowa
who came to Hot Springs to enjoy the warm spring
water baths. Because of their use, it came to be called
the Sioux City Club House for a time. It is said now that
prostitutes were available in the smaller bedrooms during that era.

A Mr. Butler purchased the guest house in 1925,
and in 1974 Marlene Akhtar and her family bought it and
made it their home until the mid 1980s. Since then, it has
become a bed and breakfast, but it is still called the Villa
Theresa Guest House.

The Villa Theresa Guest House, Hot Springs, South Dakota, 1997.

When my husband and I visited there in September of 1997, an employee graciously showed us the house, the rooms, the stairway, and the view of the building below that houses the Evans plunge, "the world's largest naturally warm spring water indoor swimming pool featuring a pebble-stone bottom, water slides, fully equipped fitness center, and outdoor pool with tube-style slide," according to a brochure available to tourists. She also told us about the incidents that spawned the ghost stories, and Susan Wall, hostess at the time, gave me permission to write my version of the stories.

Some of these ghostly happenings have been told in a story for the book *Haunted America* by Michael Norman and Beth Scott, 1994. They titled their story "Watchers on the Stairs."

The stairs and certain rooms and doors enter into the incidents the Akhtars reported, so a brief description of the historic home may be helpful. We found the house at the top of a hill. From there, one can see downtown Hot Springs and a view of the Black Hills on their south side. The town of Hot Springs is the county seat of Fall River County.

The structure itself has many rooms, beautifully renovated and redecorated by Margaret and Dick Hunter in 1990, when it was a century old. Since then, each room has its own character. One is the Oriental Room. Another is the Music Room. Others are suitably named the Royal Room, the American Indian Room, the Old West Room, the Sportsman Room, and the Tropical Suite.

The living room, also called the Great Room, is octagonal, with its ceiling two and one-half stories up from the floor and with a winding staircase around it, with a trap door at the top. The trap door opens onto a lookout, the interior of the cupola on the housetop. One can see it from the outside.

One of the strange happenings during the first years the Akhtars lived in the house was the appearance of a woman coming down the winding stairs into the living room. Though she was wearing a long, lace-trimmed gown, she didn't seem to be concerned about her footing on the stairs as she looked straight ahead. Then, suddenly, she disappeared.

Marlene told of another appearance on that stairway. As her son sat with her in the living room, he had reason to ask his mother what she stared at. At the moment she couldn't answer him. Later, she told him that the figure of a man had been sitting behind the railing partway down the stairs. She said, "He looked at me for a few seconds and then he was gone."

Marlene's son said, "Mom, I saw him, too, but his figure was sort of fuzzy. I wasn't sure what I was seeing."

Her reply was, "When I saw him, he appeared to be upset or angry. I got the feeling that he was not pleased with our living here. I didn't want to scare you, so I didn't answer you right then."

Marlene said that their dogs all acted strangely there. Sometimes they barked furiously without the family members seeing why. One time, their smallest dog was suddenly moved from on the stairway to the floor at the bottom of the stairs. He looked back up the stairs, as if someone invisible might have carried him down and set him there.

One of the guest rooms had an outside door. One night, while a friend of one of the children was staying overnight in that room, he saw the doorknob turning very, very slowly. He got up to check. When he opened the door—the one to the yard—no one was there. He never stayed in that guest room again.

Another friend stayed overnight during a snowstorm. He had a hard time sleeping that night after he saw a blue light moving around near the ceiling. He must have been aware of the saying that a blue light signals the presence of ghost.

Family members as well as relatives reported hearing noises in the lookout room and seeing a red light moving around up there, some kind of interference with work attempted there, and a fight between two figures, a man and a woman, on the stairway. That activity resulted in the woman being thrown over the banister. But before she landed on the floor below, both figures disappeared.

Margaret Hunter, who was chiefly responsible for the renovations in 1990, reported a couple of unusual happenings since then. One was experienced by the Hunters' grown son who felt that someone watched him all night long as he slept in a room that was formerly one of the "brothel rooms" off the staircase. And Margaret herself said that when they first moved in, as she and her husband slept on a mattress on the floor, she awoke to see a face above her. Later she realized it was the face of Mr. Butler, a former owner of the house.

In October of 1997, a historian who had been living in Hot Springs for over eighty years wrote to tell me that neither she nor several relatives of hers as well as other folks who either worked at the Villa Theresa Guest House or lived there for a time "ever heard or saw anything out of the ordinary." Yet, the hostess, Susan Watt, at the time of this writing, gave me permission to include the Villa Thersa Guest House stories in this collection. In fact she said, "A guest in the Tropical Room had a visit with an apparition in May of this year (1997). He saw a lovely lady pass in front of his eyes several times."

Though fewer ghosts have appeared recently, folks "in the know" aren't sure they won't return sometime just to show us they're still lurking nearby and may want to come back sometime as guests.

Bullock Hotel Stories

THE BULLOCK HOTEL IN DEADWOOD, built in 1895 by Seth Bullock, was restored almost 100 years later. The project took about two and one-half years; the rooms were ready for occupancy by July of 1991. Though the small rooms in the original arrangement were enlarged and bathrooms were added for each one, most of the original detail otherwise was kept or was recreated. The Bullock is now elegant and solid, as it was when it was built.

A booklet about the hotel and related matter reports, "The upper stories retain much of the feel of the original rooms." From what has been reported, it seems that some of the rooms also retain the feeling of Seth Bullock having been there . . . or still being there, in spirit.

Not only are there ghost stories from the hotel's past, but plenty of them from contemporary times. Not even all the pounding and painting and work within the walls eliminated that possibility.

Formerly, before Deadwood came to life again with legalized gambling, it was fairly uncommon to find

women working outside the home. If they did, they were salesladies or bank employees, "the respectable ones working at jobs that took an education," according to one woman who had worked in the Bullock a couple of years before.

Women are presently employed in housekeeping at the Bullock Hotel. Some of them didn't stay long. The following stories are among those floating around in the employee lounge in the basement of the Bullock Hotel. Some were told by former hotel guests or by former managers.

The management offered some background information: Limited legalized gambling was one year old in Deadwood, South Dakota, on November 1, 1990, 113 years after the sudden end of the poker game that cost Wild Bill Hickok his life and made Deadwood and Wild Bill famous. This was also over a hundred years after the gold rush of the 1870s to the 1890s in the Black Hills. Apparently, since those well-known events, the town went down hill as the buildings grew older and there was a decreasing interest in what the town could offer.

According to several issues of *Deadwood You Bet*, when gambling was legalized, there was hope that interest in the town would revive. The gaming would bring tourists again. It would also bring funds for restoring the old buildings and for making it "fun to live in Deadwood again."

Since then, the look of Deadwood has changed considerably. Not only are the exteriors and the basic structures of many buildings renewed, but as a tourist walks down the main streets, he sees in the front part of almost every place of business its equipment for legalized gambling. It's usually the first thing the tourist sees and hears, as visitors play the games.

But a different kind of game was also going on in Deadwood in recent years. It seems that Seth Bullock, who built the Bullock Hotel, likes to play games. Since he is no longer among the living, most people who experience his presence assume that it is his spirit that lingers. But his games are not played on the machines. Seth likes to play pranks, mischievous tricks, on guests and employees in the hotel.

One room where that happened was Room 313.

Recently an adult and a child were part of a group of guests on the third floor where these two were staying in Room 313. The bathroom door had given them trouble all day. It was an old, heavy door and it was hard to close and latch so that it would stay closed. They didn't give it much thought at first.

Whenever anyone wanted to use the bathroom, that person struggled to make the door stay shut, but it would only stick just a little. Then it would invariably swing wide open again.

By evening, the occupants of 313 were a little tired of that bathroom door. About the time the guests had stretched out on the bed to rest and watch television, they were surprised to see the bathroom door very slowly close by itself. Of course, no one had pushed it shut. It not only closed, but it also latched and stayed shut!

Seth Was Playful

TRACY DAVIS OF HOT SPRINGS had a good friend visiting her for Christmas in 1992. Her name was Rose, and she was from Boston. The occasion called for a special and very different holiday adventure.

The discussion was not long. The decision was firm. The two chose to stay at the renowned Bullock Hotel.

Reminiscent of the Victorian era in its heyday, the Bullock Hotel, on the corner of Main and Wall in Deadwood, is still elegant and charming.

Tracy had seen the television special called "Unsolved Mysteries" that had been put together in June 1992 and appeared on television in the Deadwood area that fall. It told about the Bullock Hotel and about its ghost, presumed to be the spirit of former builder and owner Seth Bullock. Tracy was so enthusiastic and excited about going there and maybe—just maybe—seeing Seth's ghost that Rose easily caught her enthusiasm. They were both intrigued by the possibility.

Tracy said later, "Rose and I had encountered such adventures before but not in South Dakota."

On Christmas Eve, then, in 1992, according to their plan, Tracy and Rose were in Deadwood and in their room at the Bullock. Tracy said she didn't have the receipt any more, but she said, "As I remember it, the room was on third floor, left center."

A spokeswoman for the hotel said, "That location would put it close to Room 313, and directly above 213. Rooms 211 and 213 are rooms where members of our housekeeping staff have experienced Seth's mischievous activities."

Tracy and Rose dressed to go out to dinner that holiday evening. Tracy wore a black cocktail dress with gold bodice design. She had packed specific earrings to wear that matched her dress. Each earring, silver and gold plated, had three dangling pieces, and the earrings were perfect with the dress.

As Tracy looked in the mirror to put them on, she noticed that the left one was missing a dangling piece. Thinking the piece might have flipped upward or to another angle, she took the earring off and examined it more closely. The piece was missing. And since it was the only pair she had along to complement the dress, she decided to wear them anyway.

"Half in jest," Tracy said later, "I remember saying, 'Oh, c'mon, Seth, don't be playful. Make my earring whole again.'"

Tracy and Rose enjoyed their dinner at Jakes at the top of the Midnight Star Casino on Main Street, the Costners' place then. Tracy obviously remembered the missing dangle as she continued to joke about it and Seth.

Back in their room later that evening, as Tracy made herself more comfortable she took her earrings off. Looking at them as she placed them in their box, she was "surprised, amused, and grateful all at once" to see that the missing piece had been restored to its place of attachment. There were, once again, three dangling pieces on each earring.

Could a person be so grateful in a like situation that she would actually thank a ghost out loud? Tracy was, and did, and said she continues to be amused by the playful spirit of Seth Bullock in the hotel that was his pride and joy and now appears to be his favorite haunt.

In fact, Tracy thought that she would probably return to the Bullock on the occasion of another friend's birthday. That would be on Halloween! "And this winter," she said, "when my friend Ros returns, we will possibly go back for another visit."

Toby Talked with the Cowboy

WHEN THE BULLOCK HOTEL MANAGEMENT gave its permission to use the stories hotel employees had told, they provided two more stories that certainly didn't negate those they had already approved. They did, in fact, reinforce some of them.

One of them happened in the summer of 1992 and concerned an older couple staying in Room 313 and their grandson "Toby."

Sometime during their stay, Toby announced, "I'm going to the bathroom now." And he did. He was in there a while, so since he was only five, Grandma eventually called out, "Toby, are you okay?"

Before Toby answered, Grandpa reached over from his chair and turned down the volume on the television. He said, "I thought I heard someone talking! And I still do, and it's not on the TV."

Grandma's call and the sudden quiet in the room brought Toby back from the bathroom. As it turned out, he had been talking—and not to himself or an imaginative friend, either.

Grandpa asked, "Toby, were you talking to some-one in there?"

Toby answered, "Yep! You bet! You got that right."

Surprised by his perfect imitation of cowboy talk, Grandma said, "But . . . but there wasn't anyone else in there!"

Grandpa gently asked, "Who were you talking to, Toby?"

Without a moment's hesitation, Toby answered, "The cowboy," just as if it happened every day.

Seth Helped Bobby Find His Room

A RECENT VISIT TO THE BULLOCK HOTEL brought another ghostly incident to light. Although Susan thought that by now Seth had left the hotel, this little story told by the woman working in the "cage" in the casino led me to believe otherwise.

She said that sometime in late 1996, a young boy came down from a room in the hotel looking for his parents. She did not remember his name, so I'll call him Bobby. He was about eight, she thought. "But after 8:00 P.M.," she told me between making change and answering questions for her customers, "children aren't allowed on the casino floor. The boy did locate his parents, but they sent him back up to their room. On his way there, he got lost, so he sat down on a landing and cried. Others coming down from their rooms saw him there and wondered why he was alone and crying."

Bobby didn't have to try making the trip downstairs again, though, because it wasn't long before someone came along and stopped to talk to him. It was a kindly person who helped him find his room.

56

Later that evening, when his parents returned to their room, Bobby was there and he was fine. He told them what had happened, how he had gotten lost. Then he said, "A nice man came along and showed me where our room was."

They were glad someone had helped their son. The next morning while they were checking out, Bobby pointed to the photo of Seth Bullock dressed in a western suit, hat, and all, on the wall near the front desk. He said excitedly, "Hey, Dad—Mom—that's the man who showed me to our room last night."

Seth Preferred Sesame Street

COLLEEN, AT ONE TIME THE HEAD HOUSEKEEPER at the Bullock, told about a rule by which her staff worked: When they went into a room to clean it, they were allowed to turn on the television to Channel 11. That channel told what was going on in Deadwood and some more of the Black Hills area. Between informative segments, there was music.

"I figured," Colleen said, "the music would keep them from getting too jumpy while they worked. Almost all of them had reported the strange feeling that someone was watching them, and some had felt unaccountable cool drafts."

As she neatly rolled the spread up over the pillows on one bed, Colleen continued. "About a year ago, there was a girl—she isn't here anymore—who went in to clean Room 314, one of those rooms assigned to her. She turned on the television to Channel 11.

"A little later, when I went in to check the room to see if it was ready for 'inspection,' as we call it," Colleen said, "Channel 11 was turned on. That was fine. But I went into the bathroom for a minute to check it, and when I went back into the room, Sesame Street was on!

"The girl said she hadn't changed the channel. She had heard about Seth, though, and she figured he liked to play with the television control and maybe liked Sesame Street better than the Channel 11 programming."

Seth Made His Own Reservations

ONE FEMALE EMPLOYEE, CINDY, had just started working in housekeeping at the Bullock. She was tending to business—the business of cleaning—cleaning Room 211.

The bathroom was almost finished. Cindy backed out on all fours as she washed up the last few inches of the tiled floor. She turned sideways, and there in the doorway to the room stood a man—not a shadow, but a real man—almost as tall as the doorframe.

He was tall and lanky and wore black jeans tucked into heavy boots. He had on a red flannel shirt. Because his head was tilted down as he looked at Cindy there on the floor, she could see the dented-in top of his black felt hat.

Cindy recalled, "I felt comfortable about his being there. He had startled me, but it was almost as if he belonged as much as I did. I never felt frightened. And he was just there for a second."

She said she got up from her kneeling position and looked again. The man no longer stood in the door-

A hallway where Seth is said to be active.

way. She walked to the room door and looked down that hallway, but there was no sign of him. And no one else was around at the time, to witness the presence of the tall man who, just a second or two before had been with her in the room.

Cindy wondered why, in all of those 24,000 square feet of building, so many unexplainable incidents had been happening in that part of the second floor. What was the significance of Rooms 211 and 213? She found herself wondering if Seth Bullock had reserved that part of second floor for himself when he was still alive.

"It seems Seth does materialize sometimes, in one form or another," management said.

The Cart Moved Uphill

ONE MORNING ABOUT FOUR MONTHS before employees of the Bullock were interviewed for the purpose of gathering ghost stories, Patty and Janet were cleaning rooms. They had been working in Room 302. As they stood talking near their supply cart, the cart freed itself from under their elbows and very slowly and silently moved three or four feet down the hall.

Patty said to Janet, "Hey, we're not done with this room yet. Why'd you push the cart?"

Janet's surprised expression showed that she had not been responsible for moving the cart.

Colleen, the head housekeeper, told their story later. She said, "We all know that the cart on the second floor would be stacked full in the early morning hours, and on those carpeted hall floors there's no way it could move alone."

"No way at all?"

"No way! Especially there, because right there the floor slopes up just a bit. But the girls told me that the cart did move. It moved away from the doorway and three or four feet, even though it was uphill."

Colleen went on to explain that in the original Bullock Hotel, there had been sixty-three rooms—small rooms, ideal as "gentlemen's rooms," with one bathroom "down the hall" on each floor. Now, after remodeling and restoration, the hotel has twenty-eight rooms. Each one is larger and has its own bathroom. The workers in the housekeeping department all know that some rooms, due to the changes, have odd shapes and angles. Some of the girls wonder if there are nooks and crannies where Seth can hide, or appear and disappear if and when he is so inclined.

But Patty and Janet didn't have time to think too long about that. If "Old Seth" was around, they couldn't do anything about it. They had more rooms to clean that morning. However, Colleen said, "Both girls were fairly well unraveled. They headed for the basement where the laundry room and housekeeping quarters are. Someone else had to finish their work for them that morning, at least until they calmed down."

Room 211 Wasn't Ready

WITHIN THE YEAR BEFORE THIS STORY SURFACED, Janet and Patty were cleaning rooms together one morning at the Bullock Hotel. They had just finished doing Room 211 and were standing at the end of the short hall, talking while they waited for someone to come and check the room. That was the procedure. When a room had been cleaned, someone referred to as "inspector" would come and check if everything involved in the cleaning task had been done properly. If the "inspector" found the room ready, it could be made available again to another guest.

As they waited, the girls were pretty relaxed because it was their last room for that morning. They would have a break in the employee lounge in the basement if the job they had done was approved.

Patty said, "Whew! I'm ready for a break. We've cleaned nonstop since seven!"

Janet responded, "You got that right! I hope there are some good doughnuts left down there."

"And I hope no one comes up with another story about Seth's ghost," Patty said. "I'd just like to relax for once."

Janet started to say something about Seth and his mischievous pranks when she heard someone coming up the stairs from first floor. Thinking it was their superior, the girls both came to attention.

But it wasn't anyone they knew . . . at least, not anyone with whom they had worked, as far as they could tell. It was a tall, lanky gentleman who came up the stairs. He walked right past them within a couple of feet of where they were standing, went straight into Room 211, and closed the door behind himself.

Startled, Janet said to Patty, "Hey—there's not s'posed to be anyone in there. The room isn't checked yet."

As soon as Patty had said, "Well—let's check him out," she knocked on the door as she thought, *Room 211 again!* No one answered, so she opened the door herself and looked in.

No one was there, not anywhere in the room or in the bathroom or closet. And the door from 211 directly into 213 was still locked, just the way they had left it.

Under her breath, because she didn't want to be heard if someone was around that wasn't supposed to be, Janet muttered, "We'd better report this." With that, they started down to the front desk.

Once down there, Janet asked the desk attendant, "Did someone rent 211 already?"

"Just a moment, please. I'll check." She looked at two lists on the counter in front of her, and said, "No, and they couldn't because it's not checked yet, so it's not on the list of ready rooms."

Neither the desk attendant nor Janet nor Patty could figure out who went into Room 211 that morning and where he went from there. The girls were full of questions and guesses. If it was Seth, they wondered, how had he come up the stairs without being seen at the desk and elevators.

After a while, they thought of one other possibility. When the hotel had been built, it had a large tin roof pediment typical of Victorian architecture, up on top of the third floor roof at the front of the building. It may originally have been a gable-shaped decoration, but in the present time it was a cupola, eight feet by eight feet. For the most part it was just an empty space or "tower room."

But the present manager of the hotel said, "There may have been access to it at one time, from 303, a corner room. Since the restoration and remodeling, however, there's no access to it at all."

But . . . would Seth need physical access?

Heather Chased a Shadow Down the Hall

ABOUT A MONTH BEFORE SHELLEY TOLD THIS STORY, she was cleaning Room 211 at the Bullock. Not alone, though. Some of the girls preferred to work in pairs rather than work in those rooms alone. They especially took that precaution, if that's what it was, when they worked in Rooms 211, 213, and a few others in that part of second floor, where objects moved by themselves or human-like figures suddenly appeared out of nowhere, or bars of soap were exchanged or turned upside down by hands other than those of living humans.

So Heather was working with Shelley that day. While Shelley cleaned the bathroom, Heather made the beds up fresh. Just as Shelley put the clean towels in place, she heard Heather suddenly rushing out of the room and down the hallway.

Shelley went out into the hall to see what Heather was doing or where she was going. Almost out of breath, Heather explained, "I saw a shadow—really tall—up on the wall."

67

"So . . . your shadow?" Shelley asked.

"Not! My own shadow was shorter than I was on that wall, so the long one had to be from someone really, really tall. I chased it down the hallway."

"Oh, yeah . . . how can you chase a shadow? And did you catch it? Where did it go?"

Heather felt a little embarrassed by Shelley's questions, but later in the day, Heather said, "I wasn't terribly scared. I don't know why I wasn't. And the other girls laughed at me, but that tall shadow was really pretty weird. I still haven't figured it out!"

"Maybe it was Seth," Shelley suggested. "He fits the description, from all I've heard and read about him. And he sort of "belongs" here in the hotel as much as we do. After all, he built this hotel himself and lived and worked here a long time . . . longer that we have, for sure."

Maybe Seth Liked Lots of Light

THE DAY AFTER SHELLEY WORKED WITH HEATHER, Amanda became Shelley's co-worker at the Bullock. The room they were cleaning had one of those bright wall lights above the doorway, just inside the door. It could be turned on by a wall switch near the door, just inside the room. And if it was one of the conveniences added during the restoration, it was one that guests would certainly appreciate as they gathered their belongings when they were ready to leave.

The light was off, though, as the girls cleaned the room. They didn't need it on, since the drapes were open all the way and the lamps were all on. They had plenty of light to make the beds up fresh and vacuum the carpeting.

Suddenly, Amanda asked, "Shelley, did you just turn this light on?"

Shelley said emphatically, "*Not on your life!*"

"Well, someone or something *did*! It was off all the while I was in there working. And I was in here, cleaning the bathroom, when it came on."

The girls checked all the possibilities. They knew that when they started in on 211, they had automatically checked the door to the adjoining room—213—and found it locked just as it was supposed to be. And they both knew that no one else was cleaning on that level, because the staff was short of help that day.

"So, who turned the light on?" was the question both girls asked at once.

They mulled that one around in their minds for the next few days. The only possibility that repeated came to their minds was that it was Seth again. For some reason, he had turned on that light for them.

Whatever the answer, Amanda hasn't cleaned Room 211 since!

The Soap Switch Scared Carla Off

CARLA HAD QUIT ABOUT TWO WEEKS before the interview during which her story came to light. What happened to scare her off was the soap switch in Room 211.

During the time Carla worked in housekeeping at the Bullock, the hotel changed from one brand of soap to another, replacing the small, wrapped guest bars of floral-scented facial soap with larger, wrapped bars of a deodorant soap. Carla had put the new bars of soap in the bathroom of 211—four bars of the same, new brand deodorant soap—two on the vanity, two on the tub. She had cleaned the bedroom and the bathroom and was almost finished setting the room up for its next guests.

She left the room for just a minute to go to the supply cart in the hall for clean towels. When she returned to 211 to place them on the rack, she found the soaps all changed. There were still four bars, but some were the old kind and some were the new brand. Some were upright the way she always placed them, but some were upside down so you couldn't read the print on the wrappers.

Carla replaced the old soap with the new kind. She put all the old bars back on the cart. When she went back into the bathroom for a final check before inspection, she found the soap all changed again. This time they were the same new bars, but they were all upside down.

It couldn't be explained. Carla had been cleaning the room all alone; there was no one else in there or in the hall. No one she could see, at least. But she remembered hearing some of the other housekeeping girls talking about old Seth, who had built the hotel long ago, and about how he came back from time to time, especially since the hotel had been restored.

Carla quit her job.

Seth, Up to His Old Tricks

THERESA WAS PUTTING IN A NORMAL DAY of work as assistant housekeeper at the Bullock. She was working in the Roosevelt Suite on second floor that day. While she was making the bed, the guest was watching television.

Suddenly the TV went off. Theresa said, "That man just glared at me as if he thought I had turned it off. But I said, 'Nope. It wasn't me.'"

The guest turned the TV on again and it was okay, so he could go on watching whatever it was he had been watching. Theresa and the housekeeping staff, of course, thought it was just Seth, up to his old tricks again, who had turned the TV off in the first place.

Monkey Business with the Lights Again!

IN ANOTHER ROOM ON ANOTHER DAY, Theresa was making the beds. "It was in Room 209," she said. Then she explained, "The light switches for the light in the entry and for the one over the sink are just inside the door. When the lights are on in a room, the switches are in the up position.

"When I first went into the room, I turned the lights on before I went about making the beds. With my back toward the door, I heard a click, but didn't think much of it. When I finished with the beds and started to leave the room, I noticed that one of the switches was down—OFF. I turned it back ON. That was a spooky thing.

"I guess in my mind I just blamed it on Seth, as usual. I made sure the switches and lights were both OFF when I was finished there that day."

74

Only a Plume of Cigar Smoke

WHEN WE LAST VISITED THE BULLOCK HOTEL, Mike Hubbard told us he had been the manager since June 1, 1998. Before he became manager, he was graveyard auditor. He explained, "I did the nighttime auditing of all the financial details involved in the business of operating the hotel."

Something fairly unexplainable happened to Mike in 1992 when he started as night auditor. He said, "I was running a credit card tape for the day's sales in the Bully's Restaurant. I was standing at the bar, with my back toward the room. There's a full-length mirror across the back of the bar there.

"Something made me look up. In that mirror I saw a tall gent with black hair and mustache. He was wearing a black hat and a long, black frock coat. As he stood by the door to the basement, he was smoking a cigar.

"I didn't think anything about it at first, because people look around in the hotel all the time. But then I saw the door to the basement closing, I shouted, 'Hey! You can't go down there!' I came around the bar and rushed downstairs. All I found was a thin plume of cigar smoke."

Mike went on with his story. "I told no one about the incident. I figured everyone would think I imagined it. Then, just about a week later, a lady who was walking on the sidewalk out in front of the building was staring down through the windows into the basement. She came in and said to me, 'Sir, do you know that there is a gentleman standing in the basement and looking around down there?'

"I asked her, 'What does he look like?'"

The woman described the gentleman as looking the same as the man Mike had seen in the mirror behind the bar: black hair and mustache, black hat, long black frock coat.

"I went down to investigate," Mike said, "but all I found down there was a thin plume of cigar smoke—again!"

Mike told us another hard-to-believe happening that he said took place much earlier, when the hotel was still being remodeled. Mike said, "The night janitor was getting supplies from the basement. As he came up the stairs, someone made his load a lot lighter—sort of lifted the boxes partially, somehow, even as the fellow carried them up the stairs. When he came to tell me about it, the janitor was white as a sheet. I figured he must have had some help from Seth."

Walter Was Despondent

An article by Curt Williams in *Deadwood You Bet* of April-May-June of 1992 explains why the Chinese nationals came to Deadwood: They came for the gold rush of the 1870s to 1890s. The town they established was called Chinatown, and it was located at the lower end of Main Street. The homes they built there were of logs from the gulch where Deadwood was developing.

Chinese had come to this country before they came to Deadwood. For a few years from 1845 on, over 200,000 left China to come to the United States. First it was for the Gold Rush in California. Some opened shops on the West Coast. Later, they came to work on the railroads. Eventually, when the excitement died down out west, many came to the Black Hills and Deadwood.

Today, tours are led through the lower Main Street level of Deadwood . . . a story *below* Main Street. When the town grew above their level, the Chinese used hidden passages, now called tunnels, to get back and forth from their homes to the businesses where they

77

cooked or set up shops of their own. They were hard-working, quiet people who were glad to be living and working in America, according to another article by Vince Coyle. From the late 1800s until 1932 when the last of these Chinese left Deadwood, these workers contributed to not only mining and railroad industries of the area, but also served as shopkeepers and leaders in the community. Today, as a part of the rejuvenation of Deadwood, Chinese New Year's celebrations held by the Chinese to drive away evil spirits are reenacted out of appreciation for the role they played in early Deadwood history.

Nevertheless, in Deadwood many years ago, the part of town inhabited by the Chinese was not frequented by respectable people. Perhaps it was because of the kinds of shops and the merchandise that was a part of the Chinese lifestyle but not approved by most European Americans. The Chinese weren't allowed on the streets after a certain hour. But they could get around by way of their tunnels, which stretched all over early Deadwood, including under the Frontier Drug Store.

There were tunnels below most buildings and streets. Some of them connected the Bullock to the Fairmont Hotel. The part of the tunnel below the street in front of the Bullock is used for storage now, but it was once a passageway by which gentlemen rooming at the respectable Bullock could travel, unseen, to visit the "ladies of the evening" available at the Fairmont down the street.

A "tunnel tour" in the present day ought to be very interesting and should bring out more information, perhaps many intriguing stories of early incidents in that part of Deadwood.

Down from the Bullock in the other direction from the Fairmont is the Franklin, also a historic and respected hotel. In fact, it has also been restored. The Franklin has one rather gruesome attraction.

"Bill," the bell captain at the Franklin, said that quite a few years ago the maintenance man, "Walter," was engaged to be married. Whether it was from the excitement of the upcoming wedding or something else he was experiencing in the maintenance room in the lower level of that building, Walter "became a bit unsettled in his mind," Bill said.

In an attempt to help him, Walter was sent to a human services center to see if he could be helped with working through his problems.

Bill said, "After a few months, Walter received a clean bill of health. He came back to his job at the Franklin, but shortly after that, his girl friend told him their engagement was off."

That was such a shock to Walter that he grew despondent. He went down to one basement area at the Franklin, held a shotgun to his mouth, and blew his brains out.

"That's why this room is sometimes referred to as the 'brain room,'" Bill said. "The stains on the cross-beams and post there in the maintenance room have been there ever since, and whether they're washed off or painted over, they always come back."

The splatters were there. I have seen them.

Some guests claim to have seen someone, perhaps Walter, walking the hallways up on third floor of the Franklin.

Bill reported, "I myself have heard footsteps late at night or at three or four in the morning. I get up and look out in the hall, but there's never anyone there that I can see. There's been no proof of anything unusual, but no proof the other way, either."

Others—sometimes these are employees, sometimes guests—say they've seen someone sitting in the rocking chair at the end of one hallway up on third floor. "Sometimes we wonder if it's the spirit of Old Seth Bullock. He built the hotel a few blocks away and then, in recent years, his spirit must have stayed here while his own hotel was being restored. He could stay here and still keep an eye on the changes. But with all the pounding and sawing and wiring and painting and all the other goings on there, he sure couldn't have found any peace over there in his old place."

People do say that the spirit of Seth Bullock, Deadwood's first sheriff, haunts the hotel built by him in 1895 and named for him. Some think that Seth also haunts an upper floor of the Franklin. Or maybe it's Walter.

Of Bloody Heads Floating

SOMETIME AROUND EASTER OF 1994, a man and his nephew visited Deadwood. The nephew was about ten. While they were in the Franklin Hotel, they found their way to the basement to the men's room.

The boy went into one stall and shut and latched the door. Almost immediately, he started pounding frantically on its walls. His uncle went over to that stall and somehow, between them and in spite of the boy's fright while the uncle shouted instructions through the door of the stall, they did get the door open. At that moment, they briefly saw a bloody head floating in the air above them, in that stall.

Other guests who saw the two frightened visitors hurriedly leaving the hotel said, "They both had dead white faces as they left—the whitest faces we ever saw on a living being."

One idea the storyteller, an employee of the Franklin in September 1998 had was that it may have been "Walter," the former janitor, putting in his appearance. Walter was believed to be the one who shot himself in the basement there, many years earlier, according to those who frequent the hotel.

A Hungry Presence

MANY FINE, OLDER HOMES STILL STAND in Lawrence County in the Northern Hills. Some others have fallen into ruin and have been forgotten. If those houses once had ghosts, they have probably either vanished by now or have filed a change of address. That wouldn't be surprising, since some of those homes were built well over a hundred years ago. The area was first developed by white men after gold was discovered in the hills in the 1870s.

In one of those older homes, one that has been carefully preserved and sometimes lets rooms out to tourists, there are some goings-on that are hard to explain. Whether these incidents have been happening for as long as the house has been standing or if they are fairly recent developments is difficult to determine.

The whole story seems to be as elusive as the presence that lurks in the house.

A tourist once asked about the details and found out that the "presence" in that house has an appetite.

LuAnn Middleton, the manager, said with a cautious sideways glance toward the kitchen and pantry, "I can only tell you what happens."

"Well, what does happen?" the tourist asked.

LuAnn's answer was, "Now, I kid you not! Buttermilk biscuits are one item on the menu here in the dining room. We bake them up fresh whenever someone orders them or for a meal that includes them, like creamed chicken on biscuits. They're sort of a house specialty, you know—one of several."

When pressed further for the details, LuAnn said, "I always bake six buttermilk biscuits at a time. They're best that way, you know, fresh out of the oven and piping hot so the butter will melt on them. And they're so good with honey, too."

"And . . . what does that have to do with the ghost or presence, or whatever you call it?"

"Well, for a while there," LuAnn went on, "every time I had six of them baked and cooling just a tad, I'd go to the dining room and refill coffee or see if everything was okay. Then I'd go back to the kitchen to get the biscuits. Several times, when I did, there were only five left on the baking sheet. Of course, I'd have to put them in a roll basket and serve them, pretending that was all there were supposed to be. Then I'd have to go back to the kitchen and bake up some more. We have a recipe we make from scratch with the shortening and dry ingredients mixed ahead of time and refrigerated, and then all we have to do is add the milk and shape them up. It really works neat that way."

The curious visitor asked whether a pet, perhaps a dog, was suspect.

LuAnn said, "A dog? We don't allow dogs in the kitchen."

"Then, what do you think happens? Who do you suppose takes that sixth biscuit?"

"All I know is, it's gone. Out of sight. And say, speaking of dogs, one night when Eva Ullman . . . she is from Nebraska . . . one night when she was staying here, she woke up once in the middle of the night. She didn't know what woke her."

"What did she think it was?"

"She said it felt like something or someone sitting on the edge of her bed, but she had come out alone that time. She thought at first that it was her dog. His name's Jim."

The tourist picked up the cue, "And was it her pet dog Jim?"

"No," LuAnn continued. "After she was wider awake and remembered where she was, Eva realized that Jim was back home, all the way down in Flats, Nebraska! Don't you think that's an odd name for a town?"

"Did anyone else observe anything unusual? Anything unexplainable?"

"Oh, yes. There was a gentleman who spent a weekend here, not so long ago. I remember him, 'cause his name was Perry Madsen, and it was hard for me to remember that. I always wanted to call him Perry Mason. But he came to the front desk, first thing that Sunday morning, and asked Katherine—she was on duty—if we had ghosts."

"Had he seen something from the supernatural?"

"I don't know for sure. Whatever he saw, I didn't see. And Katherine—that's Katherine Osgood—she helps with the management here—just looked up surprised and asked him, 'Now, what would make you ask if we have ghosts?'

"He told her, 'Because last night—actually more like one o'clock this morning—I definitely heard someone walking down the stairs. I opened my door and looked toward the staircase, but I couldn't see anyone.

But I'm sure there was someone. And when I closed the door again, I still had sort of a tingling feeling. I still felt there had been someone out there. It was real strange.'"

Of course, Katherine had tried to minimize the incident by letting the conversation end there. But she knew that he was right. She just didn't think it would help any for people in general to think that the place had a ghost. Or would that make them even more interested in checking it out for themselves? Opinion on that question seemed to be divided.

When she saw LuAnn later that Sunday, Katherine told her about her own experience shortly after Mr. Madsen had closed his door again in the wee hours of that morning. She said, "I was resting in the quiet hours, in that downstairs room near the front office. You know how close that room is to the kitchen and pantry. I sat up fast when I heard sounds coming from the kitchen. I got up and looked in to see who had just banged a cupboard door shut."

"Who was it?" LuAnn asked Katherine.

"I don't know. In fact, I didn't see anyone. I got really brave and turned on the light and moved all around in the kitchen and even peeked into the pantry, but no one was there but me. And you know that we lock all the exit doors at night. I was on duty, so I knew no one could get in without my admitting them."

Katherine had told about that incident and about her conversation that same day with LuAnn, but then she had no more to say. Neither did LuAnn. The tourist quit asking questions, as well, and left.

As she took her departure, one thought occurred to her. It would link the first tale the ladies had told her with their last one. Not very convincingly, she told herself, but she thought maybe their mysterious ghost or presence, or whatever it was, was looking for the buttermilk biscuits in that early hour.

She never did find out "the rest of the story." But shortly after that, she received a note from her friend, Tracy Davis. Tracy had written to tell her that she and a friend had rented a room at that same place, close to Halloween 1993. Although nothing actually happened that would be evidence, they definitely felt something there. Tracy wrote, "We had a room where something must have happened earlier. Maybe someone died there or some tragedy occurred in that room. No one told us, but we felt it. The 'spirit' was a presence, literally and figurativey!"

Whereas the tourist had only been there long enough to visit with the managers, Tracy's remarks made her want to rent a room—maybe every room, one by one—and find out for herself just what "literally and figuratively" meant, in this case.

Cowboy or Cook

JESSICA WAS WORKING AS A WAITRESS at the Cedar Pass Restaurant in the Badlands when she learned something about that establishment. She learned that someone—no one knew who—sometimes appeared unexpectedly and momentarily in one part or another of that property.

Before Jessica met this mysterious stranger, she had gone down to the basement level of the restaurant on an errand. The employee rest rooms were down there, and so were a number of freezers in which food supplies were kept.

Maybe because she had heard rumors, or maybe just out of habit, Jessica looked constantly from side to side and behind herself when she went down to the basement level. Whatever her reason, she said, "I was just down there for a couple minutes, if that long. I walked past the freezers to come back up. But just as I headed for the bottom step, I saw someone else down there."

The other waitresses assured Jessica that none of them had been down there right then when she was. "But," she told them, "there was someone. He was sitting on one of the chest freezers, the one closest to the stairs."

Julie said, "Well—okay—but who do you think it was, if none of us were down there? And we weren't!

"All I remember is, he was wearing a plaid shirt—it was red plaid—and he was an older man—and, yes, he was white. I'm sure of that!"

"And did he have a beard, too?"

"Hey, are you doubting me or just teasing me?" Jessica said. "I just had such a quick look at him, I didn't notice if he was bearded or not."

"Or whether he was wearing a red neckerchief or a cowboy hat either, huh? Or smelled like manure or . . . garlic?"

"Right. But I do know that when I went down, you were all up here in the dining room. And no one else was down there when I was, until that fast glance."

"Yeah? Are you sure you're sure?"

"Yes! In those five seconds, from freezer to stairs and up, there he was. That's when I saw him."

The girls had no answers for her. But not long after, Jessica was talking with a former cook from the same Cedar Pass Restaurant. He had come in for a good breakfast. After he heard her story, he told Jessica, "Why, that matches the description of the man I saw. I was asleep in my trailer out back, all alone, but when I woke up and opened my eyes, there was a man in a plaid shirt sitting there on my bed."

"No kidding!"

The former cook-turned-cowboy volunteered the rest of the story. "It was a red plaid shirt."

Somehow, Jessica felt better after that, though the mystery wasn't solved. And she kept right on looking around her, especially whenever she went to the basement. But she never saw the "man" again. Had she met the spirit of a former employee, one who lingered and sometimes materialized in a place where he had felt "at home" in real life? And had he been a cook, or was he a cowboy? Jessica is still wondering.

An Exasperating Mischief Maker

ANYONE WHO DIALS THE NUMBER of the Rushmore Resort might very well wonder whether a real person answers the phone. It might sound more like an early-day ranch hand coming a-riding in on his pony, or the resident ghost playing tricks on callers while the boss is away. At least, that's the way it struck me when I was working on this story.

Rushmore Resort and Campground is located eight miles south of Keystone on Scenic 16 A. Cherrylee Bradt, one of the owners at the time, believed that the resort had a ghost of a mischievous nature. She said, "To top it all off, it seems to be perfectly aware of the goings-on here."

It seemed that others knew about the ghost or ghosts at the resort before Cherrylee and her husband, Jack, did. One was "Junie." She said emphatically, "You got ghost, you know. Not mean ghost, just mischievous."

Junie made that comment shortly after Jaci, the Bradts' daughter, was about scared our of her shoes by

91

a very strange happening. Jaci and another employee had been working in the store when several breakable souvenirs crashed to the floor. No one had been near them, and no one could figure out what made them fall. But even more strange, nothing was broken or damaged in the least!

Numerous incidents have happened at the resort in the almost twenty years the Bradts have owned it. Cherrylee said, "The things that stand out most in my mind are things like the perfume smell in the #7 motel room. It was there on occasion and it's a wonderful scent but not one I could at the time, or since then, identify."

There were incidents that others noticed and drew to the attention of the owners. One was the washing machine turning on by itself. Another was the jukebox in the lodge playing songs when no one had put money in it. After thinking about it again, Cherrylee says, "I guess we should have paid more attention to that, to see if the mysterious music lover always chose the same songs."

She went on to explain that the lodge is their restaurant. There are windows all around the entire building. Employees would tell the Bradts that there was someone walking around in the lodge, but they never found anyone when they checked.

"We store the lawnmower, chlorine for the pool, and other items under the lodge," Cherrylee said. "Les told Jack about the day he heard someone in that storage space, and he knew it was closed, and supposedly vacant. He went up the porch steps and looked in the windows, but he saw no one."

Before Cherrylee and Jack lived at the resort, they usually drove out there on winter weekends to make sure everything was all right. One weekend, when there was snow from a previous week but no fresh snow, they found the back door wide open on each of the four staff trailer houses. Since they had definitely all been locked earlier, they first thought someone had broken in—but there were no footprints in the snow. Before they locked the doors again, they checked and found that nothing had been disturbed inside.

Two separate couples had lived in the trailer house behind the store, in two different years. They reported seeing someone there, but couldn't figure out who it was. More specifically, one of the ladies was sleeping late one morning. She heard and saw someone come into the house. Thinking it was her husband standing in the bedroom doorway, she called to him. No one answered, and when she looked again there was no one there.

The other couple saw someone standing outside the trailer as they drove up, but whoever it was had completely vanished by the time they got out of their car. The same couple reported often hearing "old fashioned music." It was always played at night.

Then there was the invisible customer who came into the store one day and went directly into the back part. Jaci and "Jim," a friend of hers, were tending the store. Jaci was in another part of the room so that Jim couldn't see her from where he sat at the counter.

When Jim called out, "Jaci, did you wait on the girl that just came in?" Jaci said, "What girl?"

Jim said, "The one who came in and went to the back of the store."

Jaci was dumbfounded. She had neither seen nor heard anyone come in. She told Jim, "But that's where I was just now, in the back part, and no one came in there."

Another mystery! They could find no one else in the store!

One of the most exasperating feats of the ghost had to do with a calculator—a moving calculator.

Cherrylee said, "I had used it earlier that day and it was still there on the table when we went back into the cabin where we were staying. But when I sat down to do the bookwork, it was gone.

"We looked all over the cabin for it. Finally I said to Jack, 'That darn ghost! You'd think it could realize we're here to stay and would quit picking on us!'

"I kept on hunting frantically for the calculator. I looked behind the door, under the counter, even in the bathroom—but it couldn't be found! Finally, when I had looked in every likely and even unlikely place, I went back to the table, and there it was, right in the middle of the table, in plain sight. The lights even blinked off and on twice as if to say, 'Gotcha that time!'"

Cherrylee thought of another startling incident. "One night we were sitting in the store with my cousin Gaye and her husband, Tom, from California. Tom is a career Navy man and a deep sea diver, certainly not a person to be afraid, and he's well trained in observation. We were telling them a few of the many things that had happened here. Tom laughed at the stories and told us that he definitely did not believe in ghosts.

"Jack said, 'I didn't either, at first. But too many of these things are unexplainable in any other way.' About the time he was in the middle of saying that, all of the brochures in a rack about five feet away from us leaped out of the rack, made a perfect arch in the air and dropped to the floor. They did not simply fall from the rack, but actually seemed to be launched. They never did it before, and they haven't done it since. Tom is now a believer and has told this story to many others."

Cherrylee was still thinking about the brochures and said, "For a minute there, nothing was so funny anymore. When we thought about what might have caused those brochures to flip out like a deck of cards

maneuvered by a player's hands—unseen in this case—
we all got a really weird feeling. I know, 'cause we were
all either feeling the backs of our necks or rubbing our
hands across our foreheads as if trying to comprehend
what had happened.

"Of the many things that have happened through
the years, some can be explained away. We had a couple working for us that had noticed several things. The
lady, 'Sally,' claimed that she was a medium. One night
after work, she and her husband and Jack and I were
visiting in the store. We told her we would like to know
more about the ghost. She went into a trance and told
us that there were four ghosts. Supposedly, there were
three men, one of them a Native American, and one
woman. According to her, we had been here long enough
and cared for the property in the right way and had
gained their acceptance.

"There is always a 'lost gold' story. Our place has
one, too. In an effort to test Sally's validity, Jack asked
her what had happened to the gold that was supposed
to be there. Without a moment's hesitation, Sally said
that the posse had killed the outlaws and taken the gold
and divided it amongst themselves, telling others it was
never recovered. Part of our property lies on the site of
an old mining town called Bismuth. Sally burst into
tears over one of the ghosts, and her husband had to
bring her out of her trance. If she was not really in a
trance, she missed her calling, as she would have to be
one of the best actresses I had ever seen. Furthermore,
she was correct in that, according to the story, the gold
was never located. But neither she nor her husband
could have known that.

"I could go on and on with stories. One time when
we and some of our staff were sitting in the store after
having just closed it for the night, we heard what we
thought were footsteps on the wooden walkway just

outside the front door. At about this same time, the two chains that hang from the locks at the tops of the doors began to swing back and forth in unison. A quick opening of the doors gave us no sign of anyone or anything. After the doors were once again closed and bolted, the chains, which are about three feet long, began their swinging motion again. That lasted for two to three minutes. We had no clue as to who was responsible.

"I might add that since we have moved out here to live at the resort full time, and at the same time assume full responsibility along with the help of our workers, we have experienced few, if any, unexplainable disturbances. It seems the ghost is satisfied that we are in control now that we live here, too. It thinks up fewer pranks to play on us to keep us alert, if that's what it was trying to do before!"

Howling the Moon

SOME PEOPLE HAVE PREMONITIONS, and others experience what have come to be called death raps. Death raps are close to premonitions but a little different, too. Something happens—like a clock falling and stopping at a certain moment. Within a short time, sometimes the next hour or day, the family is notified that a relative died at the very moment when the clock stopped.

Or, as Evelyn Mason told it, "My husband, Bob's, mother dreamt of muddy water five times; each time, the news came shortly afterward that a family member had died."

Evelyn, a historian and writer who lived in Lead at the time this story was written, recalled an experience she had when she was a young girl. Her story appeared in the *Lawrence County Centennial* of April 23, 1986, and in the *Lead Daily Call*.

According to Evelyn, one summer evening her parents were called to the bedside of her father's mother as she lay dying in the Homestake Hospital at Lead, before the hospital was torn down.

97

"I was left in the hospital waiting room," Evelyn wrote, "and after a while became bored. I thought I would step outside on the porch to better observe the Lead Main Street happenings.

"I was startled to observe below my grandmother's room a large dog howling at the top of its lungs, like a coyote howling at the moon. This is the English belief, that a howling dog near a home or wherever a person is very ill is suppposed to usher in death. My grandmother died at dawn the next morning."

ſtopey, a Protective ſpirit

STOPEY, IN ANOTHER PART OF EVELYN MASON'S ARTICLE in the *Lawrence County Centennial* referred to in the previous story, is a stope owl, a legendary character who inhabits Homestake Mine in Lead.

Mason wrote, "Sioux Indians associated the owl as being a wise bird, warning tribes of dangers approaching . . . [and perpetuated] tales of the nocturnal bird's protection handed down over many a campfire. The scouts and many other members of the Sioux nation learned to 'hoot' like an owl as a sign [to others of their people] of danger."

Mason has lived in the Black Hills all her life. Five generations of her family have been associated with tin, iron, and gold mining—four of those five generations with the Homestake Mining Company.

In researching the stope owl, Mason came up with questions: Is he a mischievous creature, or is he a protective bird that warns miners of dangers? Or is Stopey simply a scapegoat?

99

Though the stope owl legend supposedly originated in the mines of Great Britain, where Mason's grandfather Alfred Richards was a miner as was his father, Mason has heard family stories from more recent years, from the generations that worked in the Homestake Mine.

Reportedly, workers in the depths of the mine sometimes heard strange noises and voices, weird echoes, howling winds, dripping or rushing water—and while they were themselves making sounds as they work, blasting and moving rock, these other sounds made them a bit edgy. That's when they would ask, "Is Stopey watching over us, or is he playing tricks on us? Will he warn us if anything's about to go wrong?"

Mason said that her father went to work for the Homestake when he was only sixteen. His father, who was known for his Black Hills mining interests, died when Mason's father was only three.

Though he was grown enough to work in the underground mine (but not really old enough, since he had given his age as eighteen), he was thankful for the job because it enabled him to help support himself and his mother. But he never liked working underground. He had a fear or a premonition of danger, it seemed.

"Once he was coming over a rock pile on the upper level," Mason wrote, "when he was met by a pair of piercing green eyes staring back at him." Terribly frightened, at the age of sixteen, he took off to get out of there forever. Two men ran after him and convinced him it was only a big, black cat. "But my mother told me later," Mason said, "'I had to push your Dad, bucket and all, out the door and lock it to get him to go to work!'"

Later, Mason's father had a job as plant operator and ditch rider in Hanna, a very small Homestake settlement about ten miles west of Lead. Even though Hanna had only about twenty people, her father,

Edward J. Dryer, worked there about forty-five years for Homestake. He took care of the water that Homestake used as its source of drinking water and of the water it used in operating its gold mine. There, his work was outdoors, and he liked that. "He worked there for a long time for Homestake," Mason said. "I have a feeling Stopey was looking after all of us, as the miner who replaced my father was killed a short time later. Did my father have a premonition? Or did Stopey the Owl convey a warning to Dad, helping him decide to play it safe?"

Mason, who is the granddaughter, daughter, wife, and mother of Homestake workers, saw forward to the time when Lead would again take on a different look. She said, "With over a hundred years of mining gold and down to a depth of 8,000 feet, the town might change, but we hope the Homestake, the largest gold mine in the Western Hemisphere, will be here long after we are gone."

And what about Stopey? Mason thinks he will still be there, looking after the miners and their families, taking the blame for pranks played, or sitting on their shoulders as a symbol, to warn the modern-day mining prospectors of danger. A protective spirit, seeing to their safety.

A Light in the Drift

INFORMATION ABOUT THE HOMESTAKE MINING COMPANY states that it was founded in 1876 by three investors from California. The company owns the longest continuously operated gold mine in the world, right there in Lead, South Dakota, not far from Deadwood and Rapid City.

Fourteen different mining companies that used to operate in the same area previous to World War II have, since then, consolidated into the Homestake Mine.

At the time of this writing, the mine extended 8,000 feet below the surface of the Black Hills. The company also operated an open cut surface mine that was the original site of the Homestake claim. In 1993 that surface cut was being expanded and a number of houses, a church, and other structures were moved to make room for the expansion and to allow the large earth-moving equipment to function.

In the earliest years, the underground mine was lighted with candles. Later, kerosene and carbide lamps were used. Now, there are electric lights.

102

At the mine, workers are sometimes mystified by a light that would appear from nowhere. Usually, one would think a light in a drift (the miners' word for tunnel) would be needed and appreciated. In this case, however, there was no one around to turn the light on. Yet, workers found it on when they came on duty for the first shift one day.

"Jim Williams," a miner, said that the light really lit up the drift—better than usual, in fact. It was so bright and shone so far that it lit up the stope, too, where he was to work that shift.

"See," he said, "the slope is like a cave off a tunnel. That's where we have our equipment and that's where we do our work."

Later that day, when the miners found their way unexpectedly blocked by a huge boulder, Jim and his coworkers wondered if that was a special light placed there and turned on for a special reason that day, maybe to save them from an untimely, tragic end.

When they talked about it at the general office of the company in downtown Lead, they were told that some spooky things had even happened there, but only and always after dark.

For example, the paymaster was alone when he heard something. He thought it was the security guard coming through. He called out several times, but no one answered. He looked around, but no one was there.

He said, "And workers down in the computer room under part of this building have heard strange sounds, too."

To Jim, who felt some responsibility to the men with whom he worked, he said, "Don't be concerned. It'll be all right. No one's ever been hurt by those sounds—just scared a little bit."

Miners Exchange Stories

FOLKS AROUND LEAD ARE FAMILIAR with the story told by a foreman for the Homestake Mine who saw lights in the tunnels and followed them into a deadend tunnel, only to find nothing there. Others, miners and foremen and muckers who had worked in the Homestake told "Joe" the stories they had heard. Some told of their own experiences. After he heard from others about what they had seen in the mine, Joe began to wonder if their stories were all true.

One of those stories filled him in on the experience of a night shift operator preparing to do some blasting. He was killed long ago by some kind of accident, so Joe couldn't check on the story by talking with the man firsthand, but before long he had this story of his own to tell:

In February of 1997, Joe had been reading my article in a Lead newspaper. It was my request for more stories for this book. He called me on a Tuesday evening to tell me one he knew about. He said this happened several years earlier. He was working on the 3,800-foot level in a place that hadn't been worked in the years prior to his being there. In fact, according to others with whom he talked, no one had been in there for about three years, but the mine officials were thinking about going back into that area and looking for ore there.

Joe was using a diamond drill, with the bit made of diamonds and other dense material. That equipment wouldn't pulverize the ore, but would drill out a core that could be analyzed. While running the drill, he was closely watching his equipment. Suddenly he had a weird feeling, as if someone was watching him. He looked up and saw, less than six feet away, what looked a little like a misty cloud . . . but more like the silhouette of a person's head and shoulders. There were no facial features, except for heavy, white eyebrows.

Suddenly the silhouette was gone.

When Joe told his story to his fellow workers, another story surfaced. Harry said that in the same general area, a worker leaned back to relax a little as he ate his lunch. He looked up and saw something he couldn't identify. He didn't know what it was, but it scared him.

Joe said, "With new techniques and new equipment, it's no surprise that miners are sampling the area again—sometimes from deep underground, sometimes on the surface. And they never know what they might find there."

And it's no wonder that Joe and Harry and the others, especially the younger ones who weren't toughened up yet, were a little jumpy after this exchange of unexplained happenings in the area where underground and open surface mining are still going on in and around Lead.

Sally Came Back

As a result of the Homestake Mine's early operations, or perhaps as facilities near it became desirable, a Homestake Theater and a Homestake Hospital developed. The hospital has been torn down for a number of years, but for many years it served the community from right across from the Homestake Company's general offices in Lead.

One rather eerie story that has been told about the hospital centers around a young girl and is spoken of as a "true happening" and a ghost story.

During some night shifts, "Sally" had been seen walking in the halls up on second floor. That wouldn't be so unusual, if she were wearing a hospital gown and if she couldn't sleep in the unfamiliar surroundings, or if she just got out of bed to go to the bathroom or to satisfy her curiosity. But those who saw her said it wasn't as normal as that.

One former nurse at the Homestake Hospital reportedly saw Sally often. Always at night. None of the regular day shift ever saw her. Night and holiday and weekend nurses said they sometimes were surprised to see her on the hall monitor screen.

The monitor was on first floor, where the nurses' station was, but it showed the hallway on second floor. That's where they saw her, but only in black and white on the screen. So it was impossible to distinguish the color of her hair or of the loose gown she wore. As the nurses and other personnel pieced together what each had seen and heard, they came up with this theory: Sally was one of the children who died in the flu epidemic in 1918.

"So what was she doing walking the hospital halls in the 1980s?" Althea asked.

Betty's answer was, "I never saw her, but I think she could be looking for someone—maybe her family who lived nearby and came to visit her here."

Delores wasn't sure, but she thought maybe Sally could be looking for her personal belongings, like her hair brush and toothbrush. "They would have been there in her room when she died, and of course they weren't buried with her."

"But," another nurse reasoned, "if she died around 1918, she wouldn't need them now. And why would she think her things would still be here?"

"That's easy. She died here. This is where they were then. Come to think of it, she was always barefoot when I saw her wandering the halls here. And—who knows—was she buried with her shoes on or off? You never see a corpse's feet at a funeral."

Just before this story was finished, Mary Beauvais, who lived in Sturgis, said over the phone, "I was a cleaning lady when I first worked at the Homestake Hospital from 1934 to 1938. Then I went to school for specialized training and into the service, but I went back in 1949 and worked there again in other departments. The hospital was closed in 1973, and the clinic closed in 1982. All together, I had worked there about forty years.

"In 1955, I was a patient in Room 5 on second floor. I was very sick, and my aunt and the doctor and others were in the room when I saw something down the hall. It was a light at the end of the hall, and a child was moving toward the light. It wasn't a doctor or a nurse or any other adult. I kept pointing and reaching out in that direction, and my aunt asked, 'What is it, Mary? What can we get you or do for you?' I believe she thought I was in severe pain. Or maybe everyone thought I was about to die and was experiencing what is sometimes described as a bright light at the end of a tunnel, or something like that, as death approaches. But that wasn't it.

"I can still see it just as clearly, in my memory. There was the light, and a girl about eight years old was moving toward the light. As I saw her then, it seemed she had short hair and was possibly wearing a hospital gown, but not one that fit her well. I could see her shoulders. I thought she looked awfully thin. And the gown wasn't long . . . just medium length."

Now that the hospital has been torn down, where does Sally roam? Dare one hope that when her old haunt, the Homestake Hospital, was torn down, Sally lay back in her grave, finally in peace.

Eric Tired of His Own Tricks

THE HOMESTAKE THEATER, BUILT IN LEAD by the Homestake Mining Company, opened in 1914 to a crowded house. In 1968 the mining company gave it to the city when gold was thirty-five dollars an ounce, and the company needed to reduce its overhead. The theater burned down in 1984. There's nothing left of it now . . . or is there?

In mid-September of 1980, when Jamie Neely wrote a story about the Homestake Theater for the *Rapid City Journal*, some people believed that a ghost from the theater's past days existed and remained active.

The theater was old in 1980. In its earlier years of elegance, when it was called the Homestake Opera House, opera and theater and vaudeville shows were available there for the public's leisure hours. But in 1980, as audiences watched movies in the aging historic building, they sat surrounded by its antique Tiffany chandeliers, its gilt and ivory figures decorating the arch, and its peeling paint, all evidence of the era when

109

it was elegant and in its heyday. It deserved to be on the National Register of Historic Landmarks.

Before the fire that destroyed the theater in 1984, numerous incidents caused people to believe the building had a ghost, whom they eventually named Eric.

According to Neely's story, theater manager Hugh Williams had come to believe there was a ghost, too, in the seven years he had been there by 1980. So had other employees. One, the article said, was a projectionist who "felt something brush past him on the stairway, and when he reached the landing, he saw the front door open and close by itself."

Other projectionists have had unexplainable problems with the lights, or with the sound fading during movies. When there was a problem with the back-up generators shutting off and someone had to hold the switches open, not even the Black Hills Power and Light Company, the Rural Electric Association or the Homestake Mine electricians could find anything wrong, according to the same article. It's very likely some thought Eric was responsible, somehow.

After about ten days, the problem ended. Eric must have tired of his own tricks that time.

Cherubs Stood Guard, But Eric Lingered

ALTHOUGH THE ANTIQUE CHANDELIERS in the Homestake Theater were lovely, the light they gave was dim, and the shadows they cast were eerie enough to suggest a ghostly presence by themselves.

In the days of silent movies, the old Wurlitzer theater organ in the orchestra pit could sound like an organ, just as one would expect. But by using the right buttons, the person playing it could also make it sound like a piano or other musical instruments, or even like birds, or a train chugging up the hill. In the theater's last years, employees who spent time alone in the building heard the old organ playing . . . with no one at the keyboard.

According to the same *Rapid City Journal* article referred to in the previous story, former theater manager Hugh Williams said that youthful employees who planned a ghost watch at night because they had not yet met the ghost were always scared away within a half hour or so. Did the cherubs guarding the arch convey a message? Or was it Eric speaking through the cherubs?

111

In 1980 when Mr. Williams opened the building for tours a few years after the city took it over, the theater was again an attraction, but not enough that many tours were given. As a result, Williams spent some time alone in the building. He said that when he was alone there, he wasn't uncomfortable except when he went up into the attic, where he sometimes felt a little chill. And sometimes when he'd be locking up at midnight and turning off the lights, they would come back on in some other part of the building he had already secured for the night.

Eric must have liked the theater a lot to stay there so many years, but where did he go when the theater burned down? Perhaps he moved into the mining company's general headquarters, since he would feel he was a part of the family, so to speak—the Homestake family.

Spirits Cry in the Badlands

DRIVING THROUGH THE BADLANDS on the loop of Highway 240 in daylight in the 1990s, when I was collecting these stories, was an interesting and rewarding experience. I'm sure that will continue to be the case in the first decades of the present century, and for many years afterward. The contour of the land is so different from eastern South Dakota or much of southwestern Minnesota. Instead of flat grassland, much of it offers spires, dikes, castle-like formations with towers, and now and then a broad, deep fissure next to the road. Much of its present appearance is believed to be the result of years of erosion. Here and there, higher tables are flat and covered with grass. One could imagine a pleasant picnic on one of those, providing one could get up there with all the picnic gear and the participants still intact.

But at two o'clock in the morning on a moonless night, if the tourist/explorer stands at the base of one of the high points surrounded by other peaks of varying height, breadth and sharpness, the atmosphere is a lit-

113

tle different. And, if the moon shines brightly, it adds weird, spooky shadows to the setting.

Three people found themselves in just such a setting. They had started exploring together early in the evening but decided to go their separate ways before midnight. They knew the area pretty well; they had explored there before, but they don't know everything about it. Not yet. How long could they continue to find their way after a broad peak blots out the moonlight? How far could they go after they separated and there was no one else nearby . . . and the wind comes up a-howling and a-crying . . .

But it's not only the wind. And it's not a lost child. The crying and moaning is human, or reflects human experience. For the cryings and moanings heard in the Badlands are likely those of the Native Americans—the Sioux or Lakotas, as they called themselves, who once ran into the Badlands for shelter and protection.

And there's more to it than that. After the reservations were created, the government would not allow the Lakotas to perform their religious ceremonies, especially their Ghost Dance. The government officials didn't understand what the Ghost Dance was or why it was so important to the banished people. Because they didn't understand it and because they feared it was a "war" dance, they outlawed it.

To the Lakotas, the Ghost Dance was powerful. They believed it would bring back the buffalo, their sustenance for so long. They also thought it would bring back their dead relatives, many of them lost in the conflicts with the white men. And they believed it would get rid of the white men who had taken their land away from them and forced them onto reservations and into an unfamiliar way of life.

There is a story about Wovoka, a Ute Indian who had an extraordinary dream. He dreamt that the white men were gone from their land and that the buffalo had come back. His dream suggested that the Indians only had to dance according to their ways and all of these things would happen, and everything would be all right again for the red men.

The resulting Ghost Dance movement or religion, as it was called, spread to other tribes in other areas. It reached the Sioux in South Dakota in 1889 and took the form of a prophecy of a new, better world for their people. They put their faith in it and believed it would keep the whites from destroying their native culture.

The new religion bore similarities to the religion they had learned from white missionaries about a Messiah but also illustrated what had been termed misinterpretation or misapplication of those teachings. The Sioux believed a liberator would come to restore the Indian race, both living and dead; this liberator would regenerate the earth and make life good again. The buffalo would return and the white men would leave.

White men called the movement the Ghost Dance because it involved prayers to the spirits of the Indian dead. It is believed by some that the Indians were inspired by the Ghost Dance to die fighting for their dream, but it was not meant to be war dance.

The costume worn by Sioux men, women, and children during the ceremony was the Ghost Shirt. It was made of a coarse white cloth sewn with sinew and sometimes fringed on the neck and sleeve edges, sometimes having feathers attached. Pulled over the head, the shirt hung straight, Indian fashion, like a straight-cut, loose-fitting shirt worn by others today. The Sioux believed that the Great Spirit would be with them if they wore the Ghost Shirt and that it would protect them from harm by the bullets of the white men's guns.

The dancing among the Sioux began at varied times: in the morning, late in the day or in the evening and continued into the night. There were rituals followed as to ordaining the priests, painting the dancers' faces, and bathing to wash away all evil—spiritual and material.

All were expected to attend. They believed that any who stayed away would be turned to stone or punished some other way.

The dancing included times of intense excitement and action, sometimes prolonged to the point of exhaustion and periods of unconsciousness. Men and women chanted and simple songs accompanied the simple dance steps as they circled slowly to the rhythms they had learned or had, themselves, created. The dancers swayed and some fell down in trances. When they came out of their trances, some individuals told of visions they had had "in the spirit world." Others said they had seen nothing.

There were opening and closing songs as well as others, and new ones were constantly added as the dancers put their experience in the spirit world into the form of a song. The songs also contained the doctrine of the Messiah religion and reminders of their own former customs, so that they were very close in subject matter to their hearts and feelings.

In printed versions of the musical ghost songs of the Sioux, repetition of lines and revelations of visions can often be found. An example is the opening song, which refers to their messiah as "grandfather" and "father." Other songs refer to their sacred pipe or the buffalo, and some tell how the singer was greeted by a friend or relatives he had seen while in a trance. Some reflect their messiah's promise of eternal life.

When they were no longer allowed to perform their Ghost Dance on the reservations, the Lakotas started to go into the Badlands to carry it out. Though they tried, the Indian agents failed to keep the Indians at their regular work at the agencies—farming and raising stock. The Indian police could not prevent the dance, but their efforts drove many Indians away to where they could perform their Ghost Dance without the scrutiny they had on the reservations.

The moving out and the dancing went on at two sites. One was on the Cuney Table south of Scenic and between Hermosa and Sheep Mountain. This site, known as the Indian Stronghold, provided water and also security, because it was not easy for others to reach.

The moaning and howling of the wind in the Badlands today could easily be the echoes and the deep-seated expressions of sorrow, grief, pleading and praying of the Lakotas for their life that once was, and is now forever changed. Perhaps, too, the sounds increasingly represent their hope for a better life as they continue to adapt to that changed life, for it has been a real struggle for them.

Sharing with a Spirit

The Mandan and Hidatsa Indians believe that after
death their loved one is still present for four days and
nights, presumably in the form of a spirit.

"Jane," a contemporary member of a family with
Mandan and Hidatsa heritage, said, "That's one of the
reasons we have wakes, either in our homes or in
another building, such as a community hall. The wake
gives the person who has died time to say good-bye to
friends and family. It works both ways; the friends and
family also have time to bid farewell to the loved one
who died. And through that time, our younger generations learn that our people share with our spirits."

To illustrate, Jane told a story. She said,
"Grandmother—my mother's mother—died when
Mother was twelve years old. After her death, Mother at
that young age was responsible for herself and her
younger brother Tom, who was ten. At the time, they
were living at Lucky Mount in the Badlands of North
Dakota, not far from where Dickinson is now.

"Early one afternoon in mid-summer, Mother and Tom rode out on their horses to where they could pick berries and plums that found enough soil to grow there in the coulee. As they were picking berries, Tom happened to look up, and in the distance he saw what looked like a rider wearing a large cowboy hat and sitting on a strange-looking horse. What looked unreal enough to scare Tom was that the horse's mane was very long and its tail hung to the ground. It wasn't at all the way a horse should look. And whoever the rider was, he created, by his posture, the impression that he was watching them as he sat on his horse there on the hill, looking down at them."

Jane paused long enough to tell more about the house in which the two young people lived. She said, "The house was way off by itself. There weren't any neighbors for ten to fifteen miles around. It was scary enough just to drive down to it, when I was older—about twelve, I think—and we went there and saw it. The road led downward, through the trees, to the fairly isolated house.

"It was a two-story frame house. That was unusual on a reservation then, but my grandfather—my Mom's father—had been a logger and was able to build the house that way, while most of them on the rest of the reservation were simple, one-story log homes."

Then, without further explanation, Jane went on with her story. "Mom and Tom were both frightened and wondered who this man was and why he was watching them. They gathered their pails of plums and berries and got on their horses and rode home as fast as they could. When they reached the house, they went inside and stayed there, wondering all the time about the figure they had seen. Was it real—a living, human being? Was it one of the spirits about whom they had heard their elders speak?

"Still wondering, the two went up to their second-floor bedrooms that evening, but they couldn't sleep. Closer to midnight, they both heard a knock at the door. They were alone at the time; their father was in Montana working as a logger again.

"They had no electricity, but Mother took the kerosene lamp to the window. It was directly above the door, and the light from the lamp shone down at the ground near that door.

"There in front of the house, they saw the same rider who had seemed to be watching them earlier that day. This time, the horse was nearer also as it stood by the trough near the door, and they could see its mane and tail were gray with white mixed in, and both the mane and the tail reached to the ground. They could also see that the figure near their door was not a man from among the living but must be a spirit. For one thing, he seemed to be poised about two feet above the ground. And when Tom called out, 'What do you want?' whoever it was looked up, and for the first time they could see his white face in the lamplight. He was very white, or at least his face was somehow colorless. That was when Mother asked him what he wanted. He said, 'I want those plums on the table in there.'"

Jane went on, "Mother said, when she told me this story when I was about twelve, that he could only have known the plums were on the table if he really was a spirit.

"Tom turned from the window then and got his sawed-off shotgun. When he came back to the window with it, the figure looked up again. Then he smiled. That was when we were sure it was a spirit. And we knew it must be thinking, 'You can't kill me because I am already a spirit.'

"Then he went around the side of the house, sort of floating above the ground. Mother and Tom, still upstairs, heard a noise like a rushing wind, but like nothing they had heard before. They looked out again, and the 'man' was gone. So was the horse, so they figured it was safe to go outside now.

"They took a pail of plums out then, and left it by the door. Mother and Tom didn't sleep that night until it was light out again in the morning. By they were okay. They had accepted what had happened.

"When my uncle told me this same story about three years after my mother did, I realized that what they had done was to share their food with a spirit who was hungry. All he wanted was the plums he had watched them pick that day. And through this story," Jane said, "we learned that our people share with our spirits."

Peace Came in the Circle of Firelight

A long time ago, when Jane's Grandfather David was very young, his father, Crow, told him this story. Jane's grandfather remembered it for many years and, in time, told it to Jane when she was very young.

Grandfather David was one of the Mandan and Hidatsa Indians. He lived in a tepee and smoked a peacepipe with his father, Crow, and he knew the stories of his people.

This story centered around an Indian man who was out camping. Grandfather didn't know his name, so to make it easier to tell the story, he called him Joe. Joe had built his fire in a circle and had it going well enough to cook some wild game he had killed. As he sat alone by his fire, eating the meat, someone called to him from the dark, out beyond the circle of firelight.

Still holding a piece of the meat in one hand, Joe left his fire and went out toward where the voice came to him from the darkness. Apparently the other man was hungry, for the two struggled and fought over the

122

meat. Every time Joe pulled the other man, who was very large, toward the circle of firelight, the large man would suddenly appear very weak. When the larger man pulled Joe away from his fire and out toward the darkness, the big man suddenly seemed very strong.

The struggle went on for a time, with the same results. The situation changed when Joe realized he was trying to fight with a spirit. He decided to settle it. He offered some of the meat to the stranger. As the two sat there quietly, the one in the dark with some of the meat and Joe by his fire with the rest of his meat in the circle of light, peace came to both in that exchange, and the struggle stopped.

Because Joe shared his meat, the "big man"—the spirit—protected Joe for the rest of his life.

Great-grandfather Crow explained it to Grandfather David, those many years ago. "Son," he said, "remember that our people believe in spirits. This seeming stranger was a spirit. Sometimes they visit us. Sometimes they have a need. It may be that they need food, or they may need tobacco or our prayers. Remember that when we are visited by our spirits, we should take care of their needs. In this story I have told you, the spirit needed food so he could be strong again. When spirits visit us, we must take care of them. This is what the Mandan and Hidatsa believe."

Grandma's Farewell

Note: Olivia Felder, formerly of Rapid City, told this story. She told it well.

OLIVIA FELDER'S GRANDMOTHER ANNA, a full-blooded Sioux Indian, short and stocky, seemed the embodiment of contentment as she walked around the house singing and humming Indian songs.

Olivia said, "After my grandfather passed away in 1965, Grandma Anna spent her time mostly by herself at their old home in Kadoka, except when she needed to come to Rapid City to see her doctor."

When Anna developed cancer of the uterus, she had to make the ninety-five-mile trip more often to see the doctor. She never complained, even though the pain must have been severe at times.

When the doctor said he could do nothing more for Anna, Olivia and her mother, Geneva, were heart-broken. They took Grandma Anna to their home in her better times, and back to the hospital when she was feeling worse.

On their way home during those better days, Olivia tried to help Anna be content again. She asked her, "Grandma, what are you hungry for?" and then bought her whatever it was that she craved. Sometimes she asked for peanuts or watermelon. Other times it was shrimp or beef jerky. She asked for Bing cherries, too, but Olivia couldn't find any on the market right then.

During the last few months of Anna's life, her time at either the hospital or at Olivia's parents' home ranged from a week to a month. It seemed she was being transported back and forth constantly, and all the time she was growing weaker. One night, Anna got so weak that her legs collapsed under her in the bathroom. Olivia awoke to her mother's call for help. She ran up the stairs to where Grandma slept at the time and the two of them helped Anna from the bathroom back to her bed. From then on, they took turns helping her use the bedpan. She never walked again.

Anna got steadily weaker from then on, and so did her voice. One morning she told the rest of the household, in her Oglala Sioux "Lakota" language, that she had called for help all night, because she needed to use the bedpan, but no one came to help her. They hadn't heard her as they slept.

Geneva thought of something that might help. She put a small glass dinner bell on the chair next to Grandma's bed so that she could ring it when she needed help. But that dainty little dinner bell wasn't loud enough to wake the others.

Determined to find a way to help that would work, Olivia went shopping. She found what she was looking for: a long, red rope with five brass bells of different sizes tied to it. Olivia thought it resemble the kind storekeepers used to hang on their doors to signal customers coming in. She tried the bells while she was still in the store. Everyone looked up. Yes, she thought, these should do it; they make much more noise than that little glass bell does.

Olivia tied the red rope to the back of the chair that stood by Grandma's bed. She said, "Grandma, when you need to use the bedpan or want anything else, shake this rope. I think we'll all hear these bells when you ring them."

It worked. That night, everyone in the house heard the bells ring. For the rest of her time with the family, she rang the bells to get their attention.

"Grandma passed away in May 1971," Olivia wrote. "On the day we buried her, we returned home from the funeral and prepared an evening meal. Just as we sat down to eat, the bells rang out from the bedroom. Mom and I looked at each other, dumbfounded.

"My two-year-old daughter, Lisa, jumped off her chair and went running to the bedroom to see what Grandma wanted. She had heard the bells, too.

"Dad checked all the windows in the bedroom to see if a breeze could have blown in and made the brass bells ring, but the windows were all closed.

"We didn't see anything; we only heard the bells ring. I fully believe that the presence of Grandma's spirit rang the bells for one last time, to say good-bye. No one will ever convince me of anything different."

To Ease the Burden

OLIVIA FELDER EXPLAINED THAT THE SIOUX are a very spiritual people, as are most Native Americans. She said they believe that the spirits of people stay on the earth for a year after their departure from their human bodies. Then she told a story to illustrate this.

Olivia said that a few months after her grandfather passed away in 1965, her Grandmother Anna happened to be out by their woodpile raking wood chips. As she raked, Anna mourned and cried in solitude. It was still hard for her to cope with her husband being gone, and it was the natural thing for her to mourn the loss.

The woodpile was also a natural place for her to be. They still burned wood for heating their house, and in his lifetime Grandpa had spent many hours out there cutting and splitting wood. Grandma had spent many of those same hours helping, stacking the split wood or raking up the wood chips. Perhaps she felt closer to him there than on the porch or in the house.

"Suddenly," Olivia said, "as Anna raked and continued to mourn, she heard her mother's voice speak to her in the Lakota language. She said, 'That's enough, Anna. Don't cry. Everything is going to be okay.'

"Grandma looked all around, startled. There was no one else around. But she did recognize the voice of her own mother, who had passed away forty-some years earlier."

As she thought about it longer, Olivia realized that Anna was "stuck" in the grieving stage, and the spirit of Anna's mother had come to reassure her. From then on, Anna felt comforted. She knew that even if she lived as one alone, her loved ones weren't really and entirely gone. They were still with her in spirit. Just knowing that eased her burden considerably.

Aunt Lucille Came Back

ABOUT NINE YEARS BEFORE Olivia's Grandma Anna died, her Aunt Lucille died. She was survived by Olivia's Uncle Bill, their five daughters, and a son. The oldest of the children was fourteen; the youngest was only two.

About a month after the burial, Olivia was helping her Grandma Anna and her own mother, Geneva, in Lucille's house in Kadoka. She was helping get the youngest children fed.

Suddenly, the dog began whimpering. Then he barked and excitedly wagged his tail as if he recognized someone who was coming near the house.

The next minute, Geneva and Grandma saw what the dog must have been barking at. They saw a woman dressed in a navy blue duster and a white head scarf. She walked past the window of Aunt Lucille and Uncle Bill's house and continued on to the next house. There, she went inside. That house was Grandma Anna's.

Not recognizing the woman at first, Geneva and Grandma went over to Grandma's house. They checked the house thoroughly but didn't find anyone there.

129

The only clue they had was that the navy blue duster and white head scarf were the kind of clothes Aunt Lucille used to wear when she still walked among them in life. Had she stopped by to let them know she was still with them in spirit? Was she lending her support and comfort to the children and those caring for them, even though she could no longer perform her duties as their mother?

An Angry Spirit Removed

OLIVIA HAD A RELATIVE WHO certainly had something most folks lacked. Robert Quiver, her grandmother's father, had psychic powers. He said that he could see things that no one else could see as he sat outside his house in the country.

For example, he would sometimes watch his aged mother walking with the help of two walking sticks to help her along up the steep hill on her way home from wherever she had been.

Quiver told his own children and his grandchildren that he had seen her. He had watched her going painstakingly but surely up that hill. "Then, at the top," he said, "she would disappear. Not just because she started down the hill. I was seeing her spirit, after her death. And she just simply disappeared there, at the top."

He could also sense when someone was coming, although no one had given him a clue of any kind. Then, in about a half hour or so, that person would actually show up.

Unfortunately, he couldn't use his powers to help another relative of Olivia's.

Olivia's mother's first cousin Delores was an alcoholic. When she was under the influence of liquor, she would sometimes say in anger, "I'm gonna kill myself." When she drank, she became belligerent and had attempted to end her own life several times, by various methods, always when intoxicated. She wasn't like this when she didn't drink.

Olivia said, "Someone always found her in time and nursed her back to health and life."

One holiday, Delores was very angry with somebody or other. She slashed her own wrists. That time, nobody found her in time, and she died.

But . . . for several weeks after her death, at night, the family could hear her screaming and crying and pounding her fists onto the car outside. They knew her voice. They knew she was upset. They were scared.

Finally, they called the priest for help. He instructed them to burn all of Delores' clothing. Then he sprinkled holy water all around the area, both inside the house and outside.

Olivia said, "That took care of it. Her visits ended, and the family had peace again in their home in Wanblee."

Joe Had a Visitor

OLIVIA HAD ANOTHER STORY, about her grandmother's brother Joe.

"A few months after Anna died in 1971," she said, "Joe noticed someone out by Anna's woodpile. Whoever it was, and it was a woman, was using a rake. Joe thought it was Anna."

That wouldn't seem possible to most people, except it was possible to Joe and his relatives because of their beliefs.

"Joe told us that the person he saw was Grandma Anna," Olivia said. "He said she was there for just a minute, and then she was gone, but he was sure it was his sister Anna.

"The strange thing is—and it helped us believe he was right," Olivia said later, "is that she was dressed as she often was around home, in life."

Sam Came Back to Visit

DEB AND I MET AT THE CEDAR PASS RESTAURANT and Lodge
in the Badlands in early September of 1998. Cedar Pass
is very near the beginning of Loop Road 240 as one dri-
ves into the Badlands National Park at the northeast
entrance. It is just past the Ben Reifel Visitor Center
and on the way to Interior if one does not take the Loop
Road.

Deb had a story for my book, but first she
reminded me that the Oglala people believe the spirit of
the deceased person stays around through the mourn-
ing process, up to maybe a year or so. She also said that
the belongings of the deceased are kept by family members for a year before they are given away.

Then Deb said, "In 1984, my very good friend
'Sam' died as a result of a fall from the top of one of the
formations in the Badlands. It happens frequently."

After the funeral services held for Sam, Deb and
her parents went home. Deb said, "Later that day, Sam
came back to visit. I freaked out, of course. I panicked.

I went to my Mom and Dad's bedroom, and I burst out with, 'Sam's back! He's in my room!'

"Mom said, 'You go back in there and talk to him right now. And you pray for him.'

"I went back to my room, but I didn't see anything. I could just feel his presence there. And that was it—nothing more. But the very next morning, I talked with my Uncle Will. I told him that Sam came to visit after the funeral. Uncle Will said, 'He was here, too.'"

Spiritual Warrior

Adapted by permission from a story offered by Anthony Murry Eaglestaff.

IT WAS A LITTLE LIKE LIVING THROUGH IT all again . . . all the events of the past year . . . and some of them not so pleasant to remember.

Quint Cloud put the January 2 supplement to the daily paper down on his table before he locked himself in his one-room shack. He had a lot to think about. So much had happened in that one autumn month! And it was more than a year ago already!

As he tried to sort it all out in his thoughts, it occurred to him that it would be easier if he just sat down and wrote out the whole story of what had happened. He reached for a black Bic pen and a long, yellow, legal pad. He found it easy to "begin at the beginning." He knew it all started on September 21, 1989, when he heard the newscaster talking about Hurricane Hugo causing eight billion dollars worth of damage off the east coast and near Charleston, South Carolina. Before long, he had a start. He had written his opening paragraph.

Yes, Quint thought, *That was the start of it all. And the east coast is a long way off, but it was only a week later that things started happening here. Here in Rapid City. Here at the foot of the Black Hills. Right here, on Wood Avenue.*

He went on writing as he recalled each incident. There were little things that seemed insignificant at the time but now loomed in his memory as part of the whole. He felt a need to write them down.

He remembered that he was knocked out of his complacency a few days later, when he was robbed. He had been robbed before, but this was different. This time, his cable box was stolen from his TV. He remembered filling out the police report and dating it somewhere between October 6 and October 9, 1989.

What was so different? It was, after all, just a cable box. Lots of people had them, if they were lucky enough to have a TV at all. Would he miss that more than he missed the other items, stolen earlier? But this seemed symbolic somehow. Being without the cable box on the TV was a little like being without a light, like being in darkness. That same week, he had felt that something was present, in control of what was happening, but he couldn't see it. He didn't understand it.

Also the same week, Quint's friend Meredith's uncle had been attacked. He was hospitalized, and he had gone into a coma. Quint remembered praying for him as he tried to get to sleep that night. After midnight, in his own dream, Quint was standing outside, looking west. In the sky he saw movement. Clouds were slowly whirling, forming in the center of the mass a cavity or vacuum, much like a whirlwind or a whirlpool that could draw things toward it. Quint called it a vortex. It wasn't fascinating or even pleasant to look at. It was dirty white. And it made a sound like a sorrowful wailing. It was moving toward the west. After that dream, the two events seemed somehow connected in Quint's recollections—Meredith's uncle's condition and the vortex in his own dream.

He went back in memory to other events. Events so bad, so violent, that he bore down with his pen as he wrote, until the paper tore, and he had to start the paragraph again.

One friend's young son had died the same morning that Quint and Meredith had found her car missing. Hamilton, the cop that pulled up outside the shack that day, had given them quite a start when he reported, "What a day! The boy's death, a four-car collision, and some old ladies being ripped off, all in one morning! And when we found Meredith's car, where it rolled into the ditch, we saw that the windows were busted out on purpose after it rolled. Her car's a total wreck."

Quint wrote on, recalling the conversation he and Meredith had had a little later that day, over a year ago. They had just come back from a friend's funeral. He put down, "Meredith said, 'It seems like there isn't a family on this reservation that hasn't been hit one way or the other.'"

As he wrote that, Quint was asking himself, *By what? What was going on back then?* He was still sorting it out, searching for understanding.

His next paragraph recorded that not only his people, but also their white neighbors, had suffered losses from accidents in the home and on the highways. And there seemed to be more burglaries, murders, and even suicides than usual. Many young people had been involved, either as victims or perpetrators.

He wanted so badly to understand. He wrote about that late afternoon, when he had felt the need to talk to someone who could help him, when he had gone for a walk and visited his grandfather. He wrote, "Along the way, although I was passing by homes and businesses very familiar to me, everything was different. There seemed to be dark shadows everywhere . . . shadows almost as real as the people I knew, but black shadows . . . scary shadows . . . that weren't familiar at all.

"When I reached grandfather's home, I found him on the back porch, methodically dividing red willow tobacco into different pouches. Grandfather greeted me, 'Hou! I was wondering when you were going to come around.'

"I sat down next to him, and we talked. I began by bringing up all the bad things that were happening to everyone."

Quint stopped writing, the pen flipping up and down between his fingers as he thought again about what his grandfather had said that day: "Yes, I know," he said in his patient, studied way. "The spirits said to me, 'You must all watch out for the next month. In that time, there will come a power that will take hold of the weak-minded.' And so I prayed, so it wouldn't be so bad. But everyone needs to pray. Bad things could still happen, to anyone. You need to pray, too, my grandson."

Quint remembered that, as he slowly walked home, he kept his grandfather's warning in mind. And for the rest of that month, he and Meredith watched the news and wondered at all the bad things it held. When they turned off the TV and the lights at night, they heard no happy laughter as they fell asleep. Instead, they were aware of all kinds of signs of violence, almost madness, in the town around them. They heard screaming, arguing, fighting. Collisions. Shattered glass. Twisted metal.

"And," Quint wrote, "we burned sage and prayed hard for everyone we knew."

He wrote about the time when Meredith's uncle was attacked and lay in a coma in the Veterans' Administration hospital in Ft. Meade, near Sturgis. Quint had gone with Meredith to the hospital. In the waiting room, they saw others from the town—others who had a close family member or a more distant relative confined after a sudden, severe illness or a personal injury.

Quint had left Meredith there, so she would be nearby in case her uncle came back to consciousness. He himself caught a ride with his own uncle for the trip back to Rapid City, and then he walked home from his uncle's house.

As he wrote the next part of the story, Quint realized he had gone every step of the way that he could toward helping Meredith and her uncle, even if he had gone home, seeming to desert his friends. He wrote, "But I had gone home and used the gift my uncle, the medicine man, had given me, the same gift about which my grandfather had spoken.

"I seated myself cross-legged on the floor while I burned a mixture of incense in the old frying pan. I motioned to the powers with my Eagle feather. I silently said a prayer for Mer's uncle. As the spicy fragrance of the burning sage rose with the smoke, I used my hands to help it rise up into all four directions. When I finished, I put the objects all away.

"Later, when Mer came home, she said her uncle would live and that he was going to be all right.

"I remember saying, 'Thank you, Grandfather.' Before I knew he was all right and after I put the frying pan and incense away, I lay down on the couch. That was when I searched my dreams through the window of the spirit world. But my dreams were not happy ones. I saw an eerie light in the dark of night as I seemed to walk down the street. I saw dark figures next to almost every person I knew. But the dark figures had no faces.

140

"Instead of faces, each one in its particular stance and postural attitude suggested emotional upheaval of one kind or another: greed, lust, a brooding despair, insecurity, hatred, violence. I saw or felt in these shadowy figures the destruction of property and destruction of life, whether by murder or by suicide . . . all signs of evil around me.

"As I walked on, still in my dream, I saw other signs of how things were with the people. I saw one person rubbing his leg as if he had a cramp. He was trying to escape the strange, snakelike creatures that seemed to be swimming in the air and fixing on him. Another person was trying to loosen his collar so as to breathe easier—as if trying to shake off the unseen creature wrapped around his neck, as if trying to get free of the darker side of his life, or the results of giving in to it."

He stopped writing for a moment, trying to sense what that would have felt like if it had happened to him. Shuddering, he picked up the newspaper supplement again. He read the front page headline, "A year in review." He scanned the page until he found the article about Hurricane Hugo that struck off the East Coast September 21, 1989. Turning the page, he found one about the San Francisco earthquake of October 17, 1989. The articles had originally been written up in *Time* magazine.

That's when it hit him. All the terrible things that had happened in Rapid City happened between October 6 or 7 and about the middle of October the year before— between those two upheavals in nature. All kinds of recollections and thoughts and realizations tumbled onto the pages as he concluded his story.

"And that was when I finally understood. The 'power' my grandfather had told me about had caused the two natural events and everything in between. The dark shadows, the dark people were the spirits of darkness, of evil, always around us and ready to take over if we let down our defenses . . . the bad spirits that always hang around where there is a lot of drinking and drugs . . . the spirits that cause bad things to happen to people, and cause people to do bad things to others . . . just like the ugly creatures of evil . . .

"And I saw it as a whirling power that came out of nowhere and picked up speed and strength as it moved along—strength enough to cause hurricanes and earthquakes and human destruction when humans misuse nature or the environment and other humans, a power that comes like a whirlpool, like a vortex, like a mass of whirling matter drawing people into its vacuum, making them subject to its action. As if it came out of nowhere, or even from someplace like the Devil's Triangle, and took control of both Nature and Humankind along its path. The earth fights back against the abuse and pollution. It's like the legend about the Badlands: It used to be a city. The people abused the environment and created today's toxic waste—so in essence, they destroyed themselves.

"And now, a year later, after another talk with my grandfather, I believe I understand. Like he said, 'There are bad spirits that cause bad things to happen. They possess the weak and cause them to cause unhappiness.'

"I realized the need to remember his warning. He had said, 'Keep praying. And hold onto our sacred ways. It is all that stands between our people and total destruction. The vortex will taper off and disappear. But you must still pray.'

"I had been taught that prayer is a way of life with my people. When we pray we include the environment and all its elements: earth, air, water, the trees and animals as our relatives. We base our whole lives on the survival of the environment and other living beings. We see them as superior to human beings.

"An animal can survive without clothing and shelter. A human cannot. The animals provide us with food, clothing, utensils, and even our homes. Plants and trees provide us with fire, food, and even medicine. When we pick a plant, we say a prayer and offer tobacco in return. When we kill a deer or a buffalo, we say a prayer of thanksgiving to the animal for giving up its life so that we, weaker beings, may live.

"When one thinks of prayer in those terms, one develops a faith that goes beyond feeling the prayer as words. We actually know that our prayer has been answered with a yes or a no, and there is a good feeling inside. It's like a ray of hope. We know things will get better. In order for the feeling to develop, we need a lot of prayer and a lot of faith. When we pray that strongly for something, we know what the answer will be.

"When I said, 'Thank you, Grandfather' I already knew what the answer was, but I didn't let on that I did.

"My family are medicine people. We pray for those in need. We can't refuse. And we also help them find help. Knowledge comes to us from spirit people—the good spirits who watch over us. My people share their knowledge.

"From that day on, I felt as if I could see what I hadn't been able to see before, and what others couldn't see, like the dark shadows or the bad spirits. I felt that I could help others, too, as my uncle and my grandfather had, with the power of prayer and of healing. My vision had become a part of my life, a part that gave me strength and understanding, and I knew I must continue to use it to help others.

"What I now finally knew and understood, I did not have the right to keep to myself. I knew I must tell Meredith, for a start. I laid down my pen and opened the door wide so I could better listen for the sound of her footsteps on the board walk outside."

Ruth D. (Ullerich) Hein grew up in Van Horne, Iowa, the middle child of five in a Lutheran parsonage. With a Bachelor of Arts degree in Home Economics and a Master of Arts degree in English from Iowa State Teachers College (the University of Northern Iowa) at Cedar Falls, she started writing for publication after teaching high school English and creative writing for twenty-eight years, twenty-one of them in Decorah, Iowa.

Hein and her husband, Ken, live on a small acreage near Worthington, Minnesota, where she writes the historical column and other articles for the *Worthington Daily Globe*.

Her published books have been *Ghostly Tales of Northeast Iowa* (1988), *Ghostly Tales of Southwest Minnesota* (1989), *Ghostly Tales of Minnesota* (1992), *Ghostly Tales of Iowa* (1996), *"From the Face of the Earth . . ."* (1998), *More Ghostly Tales from Minnesota* (1999), and *Eggplant Sandwiches*, a book of her poems (1989).